PUFFIN CANADA

VOYAGEUR

ERIC WALTERS is the highly acclaimed and
bestselling author of over fifty novels for children
and young adults. His novels have won the Silver Birch
and Red Maple Awards three times, as well as numerous
other prizes, including the White Pine, Snow Willow,
Tiny Torgi, Ruth Schwartz, the Manitoba Young Readers
Choice, and the IODE Violet Downey Book Awards,
and have received honours from the Canadian Library
Association Book Awards, the Children's Book Centre,
and UNESCO's international award for Literature in
Service of Tolerance.

To find out more about Eric and his novels, or to
arrange for him to speak at your school, visit his
website at www.ericwalters.net.

Also by Eric Walters from Penguin Canada

The Bully Boys

The Hydrofoil Mystery

Trapped in Ice

Camp X

Royal Ransom

Run

Camp 30

Elixir

Shattered

Camp X: Fool's Gold

Sketches

The Pole

The Falls

Voyageur

ERIC WALTERS

PUFFIN
CANADA

PUFFIN CANADA

Published by the Penguin Group

Penguin Group (Canada), 90 Eglinton Avenue East, Suite 700, Toronto, Ontario, Canada
M4P 2Y3 (a division of Pearson Canada Inc.)

Penguin Group (USA) Inc., 375 Hudson Street, New York, New York 10014, U.S.A.
Penguin Books Ltd, 80 Strand, London WC2R 0RL, England
Penguin Ireland, 25 St Stephen's Green, Dublin 2, Ireland (a division of Penguin Books Ltd)
Penguin Group (Australia), 250 Camberwell Road, Camberwell, Victoria 3124, Australia
(a division of Pearson Australia Group Pty Ltd)
Penguin Books India Pvt Ltd, 11 Community Centre, Panchsheel Park, New Delhi – 110 017, India
Penguin Group (NZ), 67 Apollo Drive, Rosedale, North Shore 0632, New Zealand (a division
of Pearson New Zealand Ltd)
Penguin Books (South Africa) (Pty) Ltd, 24 Sturdee Avenue, Rosebank, Johannesburg 2196,
South Africa

Penguin Books Ltd, Registered Offices: 80 Strand, London WC2R 0RL, England

First published 2008

1 2 3 4 5 6 7 8 9 10   (WEB)

Copyright © Eric Walters, 2008

*Publisher's note: This book is a work of fiction. Names, characters, places and incidents either are
the product of the author's imagination or are used fictitiously, and any resemblance to actual persons
living or dead, events, or locales is entirely coincidental.*

Manufactured in Canada.

LIBRARY AND ARCHIVES CANADA CATALOGUING IN PUBLICATION

Walters, Eric, 1957–
Voyageur / Eric Walters.

ISBN 978-0-14-316810-2

I. Title.
PS8595.A598V69 2008   jC813'.54   C2008-902730-2

Visit the Penguin Group (Canada) website at www.penguin.ca
Special and corporate bulk purchase rates available; please see www.penguin.ca/
corporatesales or call 1-800-810-3104, ext. 477 or 474

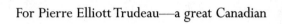
For Pierre Elliott Trudeau—a great Canadian

Voyageur

CHAPTER ONE

"BRIAN!" MY MOTHER YELLED AT ME from the front seat of the car.

I pulled off my earphones. "Yeah?"

"Just checking to see if you were still with us," she said.

"Didn't know I had much choice, since we're all in the same car," I said.

"It's just that you haven't said more than two words in the last two hours."

"Not that anyone's complaining," my little sister chimed in, sticking out her tongue at me.

"Jennie ...," my mother warned her, keeping her eyes on the road ahead. Then, "What do you think of the scenery?" she asked us. I guess it was a pretty safe bet we couldn't get into an argument about that.

"Trees, rocks, and water, followed by more trees, rocks, and water," I muttered, slumped in the back seat. I was fifteen—I was supposed to care about scenery?

"But isn't it beautiful?"

"Yeah, *right*," I said, my voice dripping with sarcasm.

"*I* think it's beautiful," my sister said. She was such a little suck.

I started to slip the headphones back over my ears.

"Brian, do you think you could put away your CD player for a while?" my mother asked. "How about if you come sit up front with me? I could really use your help with the map again."

I let out a big sigh. "I guess."

My mother slowed the car down and pulled over to the side of the road—if you could call it a road. It was more like a patch of dirt gashed out of the woods.

"I need to stretch before we go any farther," my mother said. "My back is killing me."

We all climbed out of the SUV, and our mother circled around to brace her arms against the back and stretch her muscles.

"That feels good," she said as she worked out. "This is a long drive."

"How much longer is it going to take?" Jennie asked.

My mother looked at her watch. "We've been on the road for about ten hours ... so, I'm hoping only two or three more."

"Two or three hours!" Jennie exclaimed. "I don't know if I can hold it that long."

"You've got a bladder the size of a walnut," I said, disgustedly.

"Can we stop at the next gas station?" Jennie asked.

My mother laughed. "I don't know if there's going to be a next gas station. That's why I filled up at the last one."

"They should put more gas stations up here," Jennie said.

"Why?" I asked. "It's not like there's a big demand. How long has it been since we've even seen another car?"

"We passed that pickup truck about thirty minutes ago," Mom said.

"It's strange ... being so ... so alone," Jennie said.

"Who says we're alone?" I asked, mysteriously.

"What do you mean?" Jennie looked around, slowly and anxiously.

"Who knows what's lurking behind those trees and rocks? Bears, wolves, badgers, cougars ... could be *anything*!"

My sister pressed in closer to the car. Honestly, freaking her out was like shooting fish in a barrel.

"Brian, stop trying to scare your sister."

"I'm not *trying* to scare her," I said. "Are you telling me there *aren't* bears around here?"

"I'm sure there aren't any bears."

"Let me get this straight," I said. "You're saying that in the entire wilderness of Canada there are *no* bears?"

"Well, of course there are *some* bears," she said.

"And cougars and wolves and badgers. They all live here, right?"

"I know they all live in Canada. I just don't think there are any around *here*," she said.

"Why not? We're in the middle of the wilderness, surrounded by trees, rocks, and water, *hundreds* of miles away from civilization. Where else are they going to be?" I asked, gesturing around.

"Jennie," my mother said as she wrapped an arm around her, "your brother was just joking, there's nothing to be scared of ... you don't have to cry."

Cry? I looked closer. Unbelievable. She *was* in tears!

"I'm not scared!" she said defiantly.

"Then why are you crying?" my mother asked.

"I was just thinking about ... about that *poor deer*."

"Jeeze!" I snapped. "This is getting ridiculous."

"Please, Brian," my mother said sternly. "Your sister can't help feeling a little sensitive."

"It was three hours ago, and it was just a deer!" We'd passed a dead deer on the side of the road a long way back, and Jennie had seen it and started bawling like a baby. My mother had finally had to pull the car over to console her.

"I know to you it was just an animal, Brian, but it was still a precious living thing," my mother said.

"Well, maybe it *used to be* a living—"

My mother shot me a dirty look and I shut up.

"We don't even know for sure that it was dead," she said to Jennie.

"What?" I couldn't believe what I was hearing now.

"Maybe it was just … taking a rest," she went on.

"On the side of the road, Mom?" I asked.

"Why *not* on the side of the road?" she demanded.

"Because that's just stupid!"

"Brian, please watch your language."

"But it was lying on its back with its head twisted around and—"

"The thing is, you really couldn't tell at the speed we were travelling," she said to Jennie, cutting me off. "It isn't like we stopped to check. Maybe it was just asleep."

"Yeah, right! I'm sure! And all it needs is a kiss from a fairy prince to wake it up and then it's going to join Bambi and the other deer *prancing* in the forest!"

"Do you *always* have to be so sarcastic?" my mother snapped.

"Better sarcastic than unrealistic."

She looked angry and hurt. Angry didn't bother me.

"Fine," I said. "Whatever you say."

Jennie brushed away tears with the back of her hand. Did my mother really think she was going to believe any of this? She was nine, not stupid.

"Can we get going now?" Jennie asked as she anxiously opened the back door.

"There's nothing to be scared of," my mother said, reassuringly.

"I'm not scared. I just want to go."

"One minute," I said, and started to walk away. "I've got to use *the facilities*. You see, some of us don't need to wait for a gas station. Some of us can pee standing up."

"Gross!" said Jennie.

I skittered off the gravel road and tried to push my way between the branches of two pine trees. They were so thick and close together that they wouldn't give way. I skipped over to the side and found an easier route. I had to turn sideways, though, and duck down to get under the branches of another tree. The branches were so dense that it was almost dark in there, and the ground was rough and rocky. I stumbled forward another half-dozen steps, past another clump of trees, and turned around to see if I had enough privacy.

Privacy was right. My mother and sister were completely blocked from view, and, actually, the car and road were blotted out as well. I knew they were just beyond those trees, but they could have been miles away—*hundreds* of miles away.

I looked around—nothing but a wall of trees. I wondered how far I could travel in any direction before I met another person … probably forever, because the wilderness would just swallow me whole. What a thought. There'd been more than one or two times over the last few months when I'd wanted to get away from everything, but this was a little extreme.

"I won't be long!" I yelled out.

There was no answer.

"I won't be long!" I screamed again, at the top of my lungs.

"That's okay," my mother called back.

It was good to hear her voice. Of course I knew she wasn't going to take off without me, but still, it was reassuring to know that she hadn't disappeared too.

I pulled down my zipper and started to relieve myself, but I suddenly felt incredibly vulnerable. There *could* be anything behind those bushes, behind those trees. What a way to go, mauled by a bear as I was going to the— There was a noise in the bushes to my right and I practically jumped into the air. I spun around toward the sound. Nothing. I zipped up again, trying my best not to snag anything, and rushed in a panic toward the car, looking over my shoulder the whole time. A branch slapped against my face, but I kept moving, ignoring the stinging, and stumbled out onto the road.

Jennie was still standing beside the car. She had a rock in her hand, and I watched her pitch it into the trees. Was that what I'd heard? Was that what had startled me, my stupid sister throwing rocks? I mean, one minute she was all teary-eyed over a cute animal and the next she was throwing rocks at me? No, really, that was typical, though. No big surprise. She cried a lot these days, and most of the time it was about nothing really big. And then she'd stop as quickly as she'd started. My mother was always after me to be "more sympathetic" and "more understanding" because she'd "gone through a lot." Well, we'd all gone through a lot, but you didn't see me bawling my eyes out over some stupid deer. Some stupid *dead* deer. Oh, wait, that's right, it wasn't dead—it was just sleeping, having a little nap, resting up before it went to the big deer pen in the sky.

"Could you help me check the ropes?" Mom asked.

"Yeah, sure." That I could do.

Our two canoes were tied to the roof of the SUV. I was going to paddle one, with most of our supplies, and my mother and sister would be in the other. We'd rented them before crossing the border ... like there wouldn't be any canoes in Canada.

"I tied them on good," I said, defensively. Didn't she trust me? I figured I deserved a medal at least for tying two canoes on safely.

"I know you did. I'm just afraid that these roads are so rough they might have loosened the knots."

She had a point. The bumps and holes we'd been driving over were enough to rattle the fillings right out of your teeth. I checked all the ropes, starting at the back. The first rope was still snug—it twanged when I pulled it. I examined the knots, one by one, and then moved on to the second rope. It was a little bit loose. I undid the knots, pulled the lines tighter, and retied everything. I pulled on the rope again, and this time it was good and tight. I kept checking and retying until I was convinced that those canoes wouldn't budge if we drove through a hurricane ... Now *there* was a thought I could have lived without.

"Thanks for taking care of that," my mother said.

"No problem." I just hoped I hadn't missed anything, because if the canoes fell off the car, it would all be my fault and she'd never let me forget it.

"Normally that's the sort of thing your father would have done," she said.

As if I hadn't thought of that already.

"Dad would have liked this sort of trip, wouldn't he?" Jennie said.

"He would have loved it."

"Then why didn't we ever go on canoeing trips before?" Jennie asked.

"Well, I guess at first he was waiting for you two to get older. And then business just took over, and there was never time for him to get away for long ... especially away from cellphones and pagers and computers. Wall Street stops for nobody."

My father had been a broker on Wall Street. I couldn't remember him ever taking more than three days off in a row, and even then he'd have his cellphone and laptop close at hand.

"I just wish he was here now," Jennie said, and I could hear the catch in her voice. I braced myself for the waterworks.

"We all do," Mom said. "But I guess he *is* with us ... at least in spirit." She reached out and wrapped an arm around Jennie.

I looked into our SUV through the back window. I couldn't see it underneath all our luggage and sleeping bags, but I knew he *was* with us ... in more than just spirit.

"I still don't know why we had to lug these canoes all the way from the States," I said as I gave a rope a final tug. "Didn't you think they'd have canoes in Canada?"

"I just wanted to make sure."

I knew what she *wasn't* saying—that she really needed to make sure this trip would happen. This was not a vacation for her. It was more like a mission.

We climbed back into the car, and this time I sat in the front passenger seat. Mom turned the key and the engine roared to life. We started back onto the road, and as we picked up speed, the wind rolled in through the windows.

"Isn't the air incredible!" Mom exclaimed. She took a deep breath. "Just smell it!"

"It doesn't smell like anything," I said.

"That's what I mean. It doesn't smell like cars or trucks or pollution, or food fumes from some restaurant or—"

"A restaurant would be good," Jennie said. "I'm hungry."

"Me too," I agreed.

"There are baby carrots and sandwiches and apples," Mom said. There was a big cooler on the back seat beside Jennie.

"I was hoping for *real* food," I said. "Maybe a Big Mac or some KFC, or even a Whopper with cheese."

"I'm afraid we passed the last fast-food place when we left the pavement behind. You'll have to make do with what we've got until we get to Waswanipi."

"Will they have a McDonald's there?" Jennie asked.

"I doubt it. It's going to be pretty small. A gas station, a general store, and maybe a couple of dozen houses."

"In the whole town?" Jennie asked.

"I doubt there will be more than two hundred people in the whole community. There probably aren't a thousand people within fifty miles of here in all directions."

"That's so bizarre," I said.

"That's probably what they'd say about where we live," Mom said.

"What's so bizarre about living in New York City?" I asked defensively. "It's the greatest city in the greatest country in the whole world!"

"It is pretty special. But think about it—within fifty miles of where we live, there are probably fifteen *million* people."

"Maybe even more," I said.

"You're right, maybe more. Don't you find that at least a little bit strange? All those people crowded into little boxes, side by side and stacked on top of each other, with no room between them? Do you really think people were meant to live like that?"

I shrugged. "I guess we were, since so many of us *do* live like that. Everybody comes to New York because it's such a great place to live."

"I'm not so sure about that."

"What's not to be sure of?"

"Researchers have done experiments with rats. They get all crazy when they get crowded together like that."

"Yeah, but here's the thing—we're not rats."

"People get crazy, too."

Mom slowed the car as we came to a fork in the road. Then she came to a complete stop. Normally, where we live, that would have been an invitation to another car to crash into us from behind, or for somebody to blare their horn. Here, nothing happened, nothing at all. We had about the same chance of being hit by a meteorite as we did of having another driver come along and hassling us.

"Left or right?" my mother asked.

"Isn't there a sign?" Jennie asked.

"You'd think there would be," I answered, "but if there is, I don't see it."

"Look at the map," Mom suggested.

I pulled it down from the sun visor. It was folded to our section. We had been travelling along a little brown line. I traced my finger along the line until it came to another one—a dotted brown line—leading off to the left. According to the legend, dotted brown meant that the road was seasonal, open only part of the year, during the summer. Waswanipi was at the end of the little brown dotted line. That was the road we wanted.

"We go to the left," I said.

"Are you sure?" my mother asked.

"I'm sure."

"It's just that if we go the wrong way we'll lose a lot of time and—"

"Do *you* want to look at the map?" I asked, offering it to her.

"Not me. You know my sense of direction isn't the best in the world. We never would have made it as far as the Canadian border without you navigating."

"That's for sure," I agreed. She'd spun us around at least twice and had us heading in the wrong direction as we were driving through Vermont. "So, trust me. Go to the left."

She cranked the wheel and we headed down the road.

It soon became clear what the dotted line really meant—the road was only partially there. The last road had been bad. This one was worse.

"I'm going to have to drive slower," Mom said.

"This is awful," Jennie said. "I have to go to the washroom—*bad*—and if we hit one more pothole, I don't think I'll be able to hold it."

"There's lots of bushes out there, each one offering absolute privacy, believe me. Do you want Mom to pull over?" I asked.

"I'd rather go in my pants," she moaned.

"You'd better get used to using the bushes ... unless you're planning on not going to the washroom for the next four days."

"It won't really be four days, will it, Mom?" Jennie asked.

"Not four full days. I figure less than two days down, travelling with the current, and a full two days on the way back."

"Oh, that's better, just under four days before you can go to the washroom," I said. "I'm sure you can keep your legs crossed that long."

"He's right, Jennie. You are going to have to go sometime."

"I'll do what I have to do when I have no choice. Now I have a choice," she said. "I'll wait until we get to Was ... Waswapity."

"Waswanipi, in the province of Quebec. In Cree, *Waswanipi* means 'Light over the water,'" Mom explained.

"Please could we *not* mention water?" Jennie asked.

"Okay, enough's enough. I think the time has come," Mom said. She slowed the car down and brought it to a stop slightly off to the side of the dirt track. "We're *both* going to use *the facilities*."

Jennie looked as if she was about to complain, but I was sure her bladder was now bigger than her fears. She and Mom climbed out of the car.

"Be back in a minute," Mom said.

I watched them through the rear window as they walked back down the road, searching for a good place to go. They hesitated, and then disappeared through a gap in the trees.

Bored, I clicked on the radio. There was nothing but static. I pushed button after button. Still nothing but static. I hit the search button and it raced along the dial, trying desperately to find a signal. Nothing but more static. I clicked it off again. Even radio signals didn't want to come this far. If this wasn't the end of the world, it had to be very, very close to it.

I kept wishing they'd hurry up. I didn't like sitting by myself. I especially didn't like the silence. I really liked having fifteen million people around me. Even if I didn't know them, even if some of them were dangerous, they were still people. People who could help, or at least lend you a phone so that you could get somebody else to help. Here there was nobody. I just stared out the window, watching the place where my mother and sister had disappeared, willing them to return. What would happen if they didn't? Now that was just plain stupid. People didn't just disappear ... not usually ... not like my father.

For as long as I could remember, my dad would be on his way to work before I even woke up, and he wouldn't come home until after I was in bed, asleep.

Weekdays *and* weekends. Business. It was just that way, and we had come to accept it, think of it as normal. When there was a big deal brewing, his presence was more a rumour than a fact. There'd be days without even what my sister and I called a "confirmed sighting."

Then one day he went to work and didn't come home. The police told us it was a single-car collision. His car hit a light post on the expressway. There were no skid marks. They said he probably fell asleep at the wheel. And then he never woke up again.

We went to the funeral. It was a closed casket service because of the injuries. We had to just *believe* that he was in that box. We never even saw him again. It was like he just disappeared.

I couldn't afford to have anybody else disappear. Anxiously, I climbed out of the car and started back down the road toward where my sister and mother had gone out of sight. At last I heard a rustling, and they reappeared magically from out of the trees. My anxiety disappeared. My mother waved, and I waved back, with a big smile on my face, in spite of myself.

CHAPTER TWO

THE ROAD WIDENED and became a bit less bumpy. The bush on both sides thinned out, and I could see a few scattered houses set back from the road. Actually, some were like houses—small but solid-looking— while others were more like shacks. One of them was leaning dangerously to one side. I got the feeling that if we just stopped and waited a few minutes it might tumble over before our eyes. There was a matching truck—old and rusted and up on cinder blocks—in the driveway. Back in New York, I would have guessed that somebody had ripped off the wheels. Up here, I figured they probably just rusted off.

Mom pulled the car over to the side of the road and we came to a stop in front of a small building. There wasn't much to it—just a big glass window covered with advertisements—but above the door it said "General Store." I wouldn't have ranked it that high.

"Here we are," Mom said, cheerfully.

"There really isn't much *here* here, is there?"

"Biggest settlement for fifty miles," she said as we all climbed out of the car.

I looked around. Aside from the store—which had an ancient gas pump off to the side—there couldn't have been more than a dozen houses. They were different sizes and shapes, and some were in serious need of repair. The leaning house wasn't alone. The place didn't look much like a town. It looked like something a bunch of hyperactive kids would have built—if they were *off* their medication.

Pickup trucks were parked in about half the driveways, and there were even more snowmobiles, one or two at each house. They looked a little lost, parked on patches of grass or gravel or bare ground. We were so far north now that even though it was still summer I guessed they wouldn't have to wait that long before the first snow fell.

Across from the store there was a strip of stony beach leading out to a finger of water. Five or six canoes were turned over on their sides on the shore. Apparently, Canada *did* have some canoes. My eye followed the little inlet out to open water. It grew wider and darker, and there were little whitecaps glistening in the bright sun.

"Does anybody live here?" Jennie asked.

"Of course they do."

"Then where are they?"

I realized then that my sister had a point. We hadn't seen a single person. It was obvious that people lived there, but we still hadn't seen an actual human being. It was like some sort of eerie movie about a ghost town, or a place where everybody's been killed by a virus or a murderer has systematically slaughtered the whole town, one by one, and he sits in one of the houses, watching from behind the window curtains, waiting for us to separate so he can pick us off and—

"Why don't you two wait by the car? I'll go inside and—"

"No!" I exclaimed, cutting my mother off. Both she and Jennie looked surprised by my outburst. "I mean, um, no, how about if we all go inside and get something cold to drink?" In my strange little fantasy, as long as we stayed together the murderer couldn't get us.

"There are still some drinks in the cooler, if you're thirsty."

"No, I want a *really* cold drink, like from a fridge," I said. "My treat. Seriously!"

"That's hard to turn down. Come on," Mom said.

We followed her up onto the wooden porch that fronted the store. She pushed open the big wooden screen door and it pinged, startling Jennie, who jumped backwards into me.

"It's just a bell," I snapped as I gave her a little shove through the door and into the store.

"Now *this* air I like the smell of," Jennie said as she inhaled deeply.

Finally, something I could agree with her about. The air was sweet with the smell of sugar and candy and syrup. Of course, there was always the possibility that the smell was just about to remind her of something that was going to make her start crying again. Like Dad making pancakes, or taking her to the corner store for candy. I really hoped not. I'd had just about enough of her tears.

The store had dark, wooden plank floors and high shelves stacked with canned goods. Beneath the counter were rows and rows of chocolate bars. The counter itself held plastic bins filled with penny candy and a large, ancient-looking cash register. The till was open. High above, a big ceiling fan wobbled as it turned. Just like the rest of the town, the building appeared deserted.

"Can I have some candy?" Jennie whispered.

"Why are you whispering?" Mom asked.

"I don't know," she said, still in hushed tones.

"Why isn't anybody here?" I asked.

"I'm sure *somebody's* here," Mom said. "HELLO?"

This time it wasn't just Jennie who jumped.

There was the sound of movement from the back of the store and a figure pushed through some beaded curtains. It was an old woman—no, a man—with long hair tied into a ponytail. He was Indian ... I mean Native American ... no, Native *Canadian*.

"*Bonchur*," it sounded like he said as he shuffled forward.

"Um ... we don't speak French," my mother explained.

He nodded his head. "English?"

"Americans," I said. "We speak English, but we're from the States."

"Then good afternoon," he said with a strong accent.

"Good afternoon," my mother said. "We were hoping to buy some supplies."

"You going on a canoe trip?" the old man asked.

"Yes ... how did you know?"

"I didn't figure those canoes were up there on your car for decoration."

"Oh, I didn't know you saw us drive up."

"Hard to miss. Besides," the old man said, "people don't come up here for much else. How long you gonna be gone for?"

"We think around four days," Mom said.

"Where you headed?"

"We want to paddle across Lake Kippawa into the Mattawa River, and then to Cashe Lake."

"Might be longer than four days."

"Really?" Mom said. "It isn't that far, is it?"

"Not too far. You know the route?" the old man asked.

"We have a map. It looks pretty straightforward." She turned to me. "Maybe we should take along a few extra supplies."

"Extra supplies mean extra weight," I said. I was willing to bet that he'd try to sell us stuff we didn't really need. It wasn't like he got a lot of business. "We'll be fine if we just get what we planned on."

He shrugged. "Not many people go to Cashe these days."

"We're going to the summer camp," my mother explained.

"About twenty years late for that."

"What do you mean?"

"It's all closed down."

"It isn't operating anymore?"

My mother sounded really disappointed. I felt the opposite. No camp meant no canoe trip, and we could head back to the city.

"That's sad," she said. "My husband always spoke so fondly of his summers there."

"Lots of people passed through that camp. All that's left are the remains of the cabins ... pretty rundown, pretty overgrown."

"Does that mean we're not going?" Jennie asked.

"No, we're going," my mother said, very definitely.

My heart and hopes sank.

"But if there's no camp, where will we sleep?" Jennie asked.

"You can still stay there," the old man said. "It's not like there's anybody to chase you away."

"But you said it was abandoned," I said.

"It is. But you can still camp."

"Besides, it's not the camp that's important," my mother said, "it's the lake. That's why we're going."

I wanted to argue—heck, I'd argued about this trip for weeks—but I'd learned that my mother had made up her mind, and nothing was going to change it. This trip was really, really important for her.

"Lots of people still come up to see the camp," the old man went on. "People who spent time there as kids. Must have been a good place."

"My husband said he spent some of the happiest times of his life there."

The old man looked at my mother, then me, then my sister. "Just three of you, right?"

My mother nodded. "My husband died this spring in a car accident."

"Sorry to hear … things happen … don't always see the reason," the old man said.

We all stood there awkwardly, staring down at our feet. Why did she have to tell him? Why did she have to tell everybody? It didn't help. It just made us sad and the person she told uncomfortable.

"Here's a list of the supplies we still need." She pulled out a piece of paper, unfolded it, and handed it to the man.

He ran a shaking finger slowly down the list. "We got everything."

"Maybe you can add a few extra things," I said, meekly. "You know, because the camp isn't there anymore."

"Will do. You setting off in the morning?"

"We thought we'd go right away, paddle for a few hours, and then set in to shore and camp for the night," my mother said.

"Lots of spots to camp. Let's get to that list so you can get out on the water."

"I appreciate that. Would it be possible for us to leave our car here somewhere for a few days?"

"Just pull it around to the back of the store. Nobody will bother it."

Yeah, right! I thought. I wouldn't have left our SUV alone and unwatched for more than five minutes in the city, much less four days. I'd have come back to find the CD player ripped right out of the dash ... at least! But my mother didn't see it that way.

"Thank you so much," she said.

THE BLADE OF THE PADDLE slipped into the water with barely a splash. I paddled two strokes on one side and then two on the other, keeping the canoe moving straight and strong, just the way I'd learned at camp, Camp Kelso. It was in the Adirondacks, up in "the *wilderness*." That was how the brochure described it, but it wasn't really that wild. There were cottages everywhere, and motorboats crisscrossed the lake, and there were stores and villages and towns nearby. If the wind was blowing in the right direction you could even smell the McDonald's out on Route 6. Or maybe it was the Burger King, or the Wendy's. If you wanted to, you could sneak out of camp—which my friends and I frequently did—grab a burger, and shop at some outlet stores, or at the place that sold Native American souvenirs ... made in China. There was even a bowling alley on the highway. I liked the bowling alley. It had a great video arcade.

Okay, so maybe it wasn't the real wilderness, but compared to New York City it *was* the middle of nowhere. Until this summer, I'd spent a couple of weeks up there every year since I was eight. What with everything that had happened, we'd all just stayed at home so far this summer, sitting around, doing nothing but thinking, or trying hard not to think about anything at all. Waiting. Killing time. Somehow that seemed right— killing time. Waiting for time to heal us. I didn't think I'd ever live long enough for that to happen. But at least I wasn't crying all the time like my sister, or pretending that everything was all right like my mother.

Camp Kelso had been my father's idea. He'd wanted me to learn how to swim up there, and how to canoe. Those weren't the sorts of things you could do in New York City, unless you were going to swim in the East River or take a paddleboat around the reservoir in Central Park.

I remember that first summer, being driven up to camp and really, really not wanting to go. I begged them not to leave me. I didn't know how I could survive without my parents right there. I fought hard to hold back the tears as they left. I can still picture them in the car, my father at the wheel, my mother in tears beside him, my sister strapped into a car seat in the back, waving as they drove away. I felt so scared, so alone, so abandoned.

If I were writing a short story, I guess I'd say that I finally learned to love camp and couldn't wait to get back the next summer. But that's not how it really happened. It rained, I hated it, I got sunburned, and I couldn't sleep because of all the nature noises in the woods. But I did go back, every year. I got over my homesickness. I made friends with a bunch of the guys, and that was a big part of it. But I also went because I didn't want to disappoint my father. He was always talking about Cashe Lake, and about how the camping and canoeing were *his* best memories of growing up. I kept giving it a try, for his sake.

Of course, he didn't grow up in New York. His family was from Montreal, Canada, and that's where he was raised. They lived in a little tenement—a second-storey walk-up—him, his mother, and his father. No brothers or sisters. His parents, my grandparents, didn't have much money—certainly not enough to pay for any camp. The one my father went to was run by a charity that wanted to send poor inner-city kids up north. That's what he was, a poor inner-city kid. I always thought that was why he worked so hard to make a lot of money. He didn't want to be poor again, ever, and he didn't want us to have to go through what he'd gone through.

Once, long before my sister and I were even born, my father mentioned to my mother that when he died he wanted his ashes scattered at the lake where he'd spent his childhood summers. He was probably just joking around—who ever thinks they're really going to die?—but she remembered. And now we were paddling our canoes toward that lake.

At the front of my canoe, along with a tent and sleeping bags and supplies piled on top, was the urn holding his ashes. Here we were, just the two of us, riding along together in a canoe. He'd talked about doing that, the four of us going on a canoe trip, but there'd never been time. There was always some deal that needed to be chased down, some client who had to be satisfied, money that needed to be made. Like any of that made any difference now. But anyway, here we were at last, riding together in a canoe, just like he'd wanted ... well, maybe not *exactly* like he'd wanted ... not exactly the way anybody would want.

Despite everything, it did feel kind of good to be out on the water, away from everything and everybody. I liked being by myself. The only thing that was getting on my nerves, aside from the blisters I could already feel starting on my palms, was the silence. Except for the sound of the water and the wind, there was complete silence. I wasn't used to that. Camp Kelso had been quiet, but not like this. There, you could often hear a powerboat or a jet-ski roaring in the distance, or see a plane overhead, or overhear voices or music floating across the water. It was amazing how far sound travelled over the water, especially at night. Here, there was just the wind, and the water. "What do you think?" I asked the ashes in the hidden urn. "Beautiful day, huh?" I waited for his answer. "I guess you'd rather paddle than talk. Then again, I seem to be doing all the paddling here. Maybe we both need a rest."

I lifted the paddle and rested it across the gunwales of the canoe. Maybe I really did need a rest. After all, making bad jokes about my dead father *and* talking to his ashes—those had to be two serious signs of mental illness.

It wasn't *my* mental health that I was that worried about, though. My mother had cried for days and days after my father died, until I began to wonder if the tears would ever end. Then, like some switch had been flipped, she'd stopped crying and got really cheerful and positive. *Too* cheerful and positive. It felt fake, like she was trying way too hard to deny that anything was wrong. She was still kind of like that. I'd have liked it better if she'd been just a little less chipper. It was kind of freaking me out.

"You want something to drink?" I asked my father's ashes.

There was no answer except the lapping of the waves against the fibreglass canoe. I took that to mean no. I reached down for the canteen, opened it, and took a big swig.

"You sure? It's cold and—"

"Did you say something?" my mother called out.

I startled and turned around. She and Jennie had crept up on me while I was resting, and they were only a few canoe lengths behind me now. My mother was a really strong paddler. She'd even paddled on a dragon-boat team just for fun when she was in college. I guess some skills just stayed with you.

"What did you say?" Mom repeated.

"Nothing," I mumbled, "just getting a drink. How soon are we going to put in for the night?"

"I was thinking pretty soon. How about if you keep your eyes open for a good spot and we'll camp there."

"I'll watch." I screwed the lid back on the canteen, dropped it at my feet, and started paddling again.

CHAPTER THREE

I STAYED CLOSE TO THE SHORE, hoping to find the right spot to camp. I needed a place that was shallow enough to beach the canoes but that had a big enough clearing to pitch the tent. The old man in the store had said we'd find plenty of places. Well, not that I could see. The bush was thick and generally came right down to the edge of the water. And if there weren't trees, there was solid rock. How was I going to pitch a tent if I had to drive the tent pegs into solid rock?

The sun was getting lower in the sky. It was late—almost ten—but we were so far north that we'd have light until almost eleven. Still, that left us only an hour to find a spot, set up camp, eat, and get to sleep before dark. I was hungry and tired and I really wanted to stop paddling. My arms were burning. We'd been canoeing straight into a strong headwind. This was nothing at all like doing a few lazy laps around that little lake at camp, knowing that if the worst came to the worst they'd send out a motorboat to tow us in.

Up ahead I spied what looked like a potential campsite. It wasn't on shore, it was on a little island, but it appeared to have a shallow beach to land on. I paddled harder on the left side and steered the canoe to the left, toward the island. The closer I got, the better it looked. There was a clearing—some rock, but definitely some open ground, and a little bit of sand running along the water. The canoe glided forward until it scraped against the bottom. I'd have to get out and drag it the rest of the way in.

I pulled myself up from my knees and balanced on the seat just long enough to remove my running shoes and socks. Then I distributed my weight with my hands on the gunwales so I wouldn't tip the canoe and quickly jumped out sideways. My feet sank into soft, gunky, gooey mud. I walked to shore, dragging the canoe with me up onto the little beach. I didn't stop until I'd pulled the canoe entirely out of the water.

Looking back, I could see my mother and sister still out on the lake. Their red life jackets made them easy to spot. I waved my hands above my head and my sister waved back.

There was no time to waste. I needed to unload my canoe and set up camp. I was hoping to get everything ready before they joined me. I pulled out the bright red nylon bag that held the tent. We'd been thinking mostly about staying in the cabins at the camp, but as we were driving through Montreal, my mother had suddenly remembered that we'd need to camp along the way until we got there, so we'd stopped at a sporting goods store and purchased the tent.

I loosened the drawstring, opened the bag, and dumped the contents out. I picked up the tent, also bright red nylon. It was tightly bound up and I spread it out on the ground. It was supposed to be a four-man tent but it looked bigger than that. I smoothed it out so that it was sitting on its bottom. The ground was pretty flat. This was probably as good a spot as anyplace else.

There it was, the little plastic bag that held the tent pegs. I ripped it open with my teeth and dumped the pegs out onto the ground. Twelve pegs—one for each corner, one for the middle of each side, and one for each of the four guy ropes. I had set up tents before at camp so I had a pretty good idea how to do it. I'd drive in the pegs at the four corners first and then work from there. This wouldn't be too tricky. All I needed was a hammer ... okay, did we have a hammer? Probably not, but a rock would do just as well. I scrambled over on my knees and grabbed a rock that was about the right size and weight.

I put the first peg through the loop and, careful not to bang my fingers, tapped the rock against the peg. It sank in easily. I tapped it a second and third and fourth time and it snugged into the loop of the tent. I repeated the process for the other three corners. This was looking pretty easy. Before I did the rest of the floor pegs or set up the guy ropes I'd just slip in the poles and … the poles … where were the poles? I looked around. I didn't see them anywhere. I grabbed the bag—the *empty* bag. Maybe they were underneath the floor of the tent. I felt around. There were a couple of small rocks trapped beneath the nylon—I should have cleared them away before I put in the pegs—but there were no poles. There *had* to be poles … unless this was some special type of tent that didn't need poles.

Instructions … I needed the instructions. I looked around. A little scrap of paper had fallen out of the bag when I'd dumped it looking for the poles. Now, where was it? There it was, just off to the side. It must have blown there. I scrambled over, picked up the paper, and looked. At the top of the page, in big bold letters, it said "INSTRUCTIONS." Beautiful! At least this would tell me … it was written in some foreign language … French, or maybe Spanish. No, I could read a little Spanish and this wasn't it. English had to be on the back. I flipped it over. But whatever language was there certainly wasn't English. It was Chinese or Japanese or some other stupid language that used squiggles and pictures to make up words. Great!

Along with the squiggles there were diagrams, though. And in those diagrams were poles—the poles you needed to set up the tent. Poles that I didn't have. How could I set up a tent without—?

"AAAAHHH!"

I jumped up and spun around. At first all I saw was the bright red bottom of a canoe. Then my mother and sister appeared, soaking wet, getting to their feet in the shallow water. I ran over and waded in to help them.

"What happened?" I yelled.

"We were just trying to get out and we tipped it," my mother said. "Stupid."

I grabbed the canoe and flipped it over. The bottom was filled with water. All of the contents of the canoe had been dumped out and were either floating on the surface or had sunk into the muck on the bottom.

We all scrambled to retrieve things. I grabbed one of their packs—partially submerged and, judging by the weight, soaked right through—and tossed it onto the shore. My mother grabbed the two sleeping bags, and water ran out of them as she held them up. She swung them toward land, but one bounced up onto the sand while the other just rolled back into the water. My sister dragged her pack behind her as she waded out of the water and then flopped down on the little beach, moaning. There were still a couple of pots floating and some food supplies. I caught sight of something glittering in the mud. I reached down carefully and pulled out the hatchet.

"I think that's everything," my mother said.

I dragged the second canoe up out of the lake. With all the water in the bottom it was pretty heavy. As soon as I could, I tipped it to one side to allow the water to drain out, and then I dragged it farther up, completely out of the water.

"We'd better make a fire and dry everything out … or at least the sleeping bags," my mother said.

I picked up the hatchet. "I'll get some firewood."

"That's great. A big, roaring fire will dry everything off and feel … wait … the matches." My mother opened the straps on her pack and started to pull things out. She held up a cardboard box—a box of matches. She opened it, tipped it to the side, and water poured out.

"I don't think we're going to be having a fire tonight," she said.

"Are those are only matches?" I asked in disbelief.

"It's a big box … I didn't think we'd need even this many so I didn't think to pack—"

"Didn't you think about maybe putting them in a waterproof container?" I demanded.

She shrugged. "Sorry."

"Great. Wet sleeping bags, wet clothes, no matches to make a fire, and we don't have a tent."

"No tent? But wasn't the tent in your canoe?"

"The tent was. The poles weren't. There were no poles in the bag."

"But there *have* to be poles!"

"There are none. They weren't included, or they forgot to give them to us. Either way, we don't have any tent poles."

My mother started to say something—her mouth opened and then closed. She looked like she was going to cry. I was almost happy about that. At least she wasn't going to give us some happy message about how wonderful it was all going to be. On the other hand, if she started to cry, I could only imagine what Jennie would do. I had to say something fast ... something positive.

"Look, we still have one dry sleeping bag. We'll lay the other two out and they'll be dry by morning. We'll do the same with the clothes, and you two can change into some of my extra stuff. At least *I* know how to get out of a canoe without tipping it." Okay, that was a cheap shot. "The clothes won't fit great, but it's not like there's anybody here to see. And I bet we can use the guy ropes to hold the tent up even if we don't have any poles. It'll be all right."

My mother smiled. "That's just like you. Always looking for solutions." She wrapped her arms around me and gave me a big, damp hug.

"We'll do just fine," I said, though I wasn't sure I believed it. "This is nothing. Nothing at all."

I LOOKED UP AT THE NIGHT SKY. It was filled with thousands and thousands and thousands of stars. I just lay there on the ground staring up. I knew it was basically the same sky that stretched out over my head every night in New York, but it seemed so different. In the city, all the illumination from street lights and houses and apartments and cars blotted out the faint light coming from the heavens. Here, where there was no other light, the stars were a mass of pinpoints in the jet-black sky.

"Are you asleep?"

It was my mother. I sat up.

"No," I said, shaking my head. "Is Jennie awake?"

"She fell asleep the second she snuggled into your sleeping bag. That was very nice of you," she said.

"I'm feeling pretty warm without it." I'd put a big, warm, fuzzy hoodie over my T-shirt. My mother and sister had both changed into the clothing I had left over.

"How's the tent holding out?"

"Not bad at all," she said.

I'd moved it close to some small evergreen trees and tied the ropes around the branches so the sides and roof would be held up.

"There's room in there for all three of us," my mother pointed out.

"That's okay. I like it out here." I was using the overturned canoe as my shelter. It was like a little house.

"You certainly picked a lovely place to put in for the night," she said.

"It looked like a good spot."

"It was an interesting choice," my mother said. "I don't think I've ever slept on an island before," she added.

I gave her a questioning look. "We *always* sleep on an island ... the Island of Manhattan."

She chuckled. "This is just a *little* different."

Since setting up camp I'd been thinking about the advantages of being on an island, how it was a safe spot. This little outcrop of rock and roots and dirt was separate from the mainland, and there were no bears or wolves or anything else out here. We were safe. Of course, some animals *could* swim ...

"Your father would have loved to have been here."

"It is a nice spot."

"I mean up here ... on this lake ... up in Canada."

"If he liked Canada so much, then why didn't we ever come up here?" I asked.

"I guess there just wasn't enough time. Before you were born we'd come up to Montreal to see his parents, your grandparents. We always spent part of our Christmas holidays and some of each summer up here. And then first your grandfather died, and three months later your grandmother passed away. After that, there just weren't the same reasons for us to come up. It would have been different if your father had had brothers and sisters."

"Yeah, then we would have had uncles and aunts and cousins, even," I added. Both my parents were the only kids in their families. We'd been close to my mom's parents, too, my Nana and Papa, but they had both died as well. We didn't have a lot of family left.

"I think your father had some more distant relatives ... sort of second or third cousins. And Martin is a very common name in Quebec, although they pronounce it Mar-*tan*."

"That makes it sound French. Dad wasn't French."

"No, but he did grow up in a French-Canadian neighbourhood, and he could certainly speak French very well."

"It always sounded funny when he spoke French."

"I wish he'd taught you and your sister to speak it," Mom said.

"Why?"

"A second language is always a good thing to have."

"A second language maybe, but French? Wouldn't it make more sense to learn Spanish?"

"Living in New York, Spanish makes more sense, but French would be better here. Knowing French might have helped keep us from getting lost!"

She was right. All the way through Quebec, the highway signs and all the billboards and store signs had all been in French. And even the tent instructions! But then again, being able to read French wouldn't have helped nearly as much as having a set of tent poles.

"We should turn in soon, it's getting late," my mother pointed out. "After all, we're a lot farther north here than in New York. The summer days are long. It's already after midnight. Are you hungry?" she asked.

"A little. You?"

"A little. Cereal didn't quite do the job."

Without a fire we hadn't been able to heat anything up, so my mother had opened up a box of cereal—the cereal had stayed dry because it was still sealed in its bag inside the box—and we'd eaten that for supper.

"Hopefully some of the matches will be dry by morning and we'll be able to have a warm breakfast. Maybe some oatmeal."

"Now *that's* something to look forward to," I said, sarcastically.

"Get to sleep," she said, with a chuckle.

"I'll try."

She got up and took a few steps and then stopped and turned around. "Brian?"

"Yeah?"

"Thanks. Thanks for being there."

"It was just a sleeping bag," I mumbled, rolling over and closing my eyes.

"I didn't mean just tonight. I don't know how I could have gotten through the last three months without you."

I wanted to tell her it was okay, or "No problem," or something. Instead I said nothing.

CHAPTER FOUR

I WASN'T SURE WHAT WAS SCREAMING at me the loudest—the ache in my back, the grumbling in my stomach, the blisters on my hands, or the burning in my arms as I paddled. I was sore, tired, hungry, and in a particularly foul mood. On the bright side, the wind had shifted around so it was at our backs, pushing us across the water.

Stretched across the bow of the canoe were some of my sister's clothing and her sleeping bag, partially open, still damp, drying in the wind and sun. She'd better have been hoping that hers would be dry by nightfall, because I wasn't planning on sleeping without one again. It had gotten really cold last night and I'd woken up at least a dozen times, shivering. I never really slept very well, even in my own bed, but shivering in the cold had added a nightmarish quality.

We were paddling just out from the shore. It would have been faster and a lot shorter to just cut across Lake Kippawa to the mouth of the Mattawa—that is, if we'd known exactly where the mouth of the river *was*. The map wasn't big enough to show much detail, and now, out on the water, it didn't help at all. All we could do was stay close to the shore until we found it. If we missed it, we might end up going halfway around the lake before we figured out we had to turn back around. I had a sickening thought: what if we'd missed it already? When we'd planned out this trip, my mother and I had figured that we could get to the mouth of the river on the first day. Now here we were, four hours into the second day, and still no river in sight.

I looked back over my shoulder. My mother and sister were well behind me. Maybe if they could have kept up, we would have been there by now. I needed a break. I needed a rest. I needed lunch. Cold cereal and an apple wasn't much of a breakfast. All I had to munch on now were granola bars and something called "trail mix"—a strange combination of nuts and raisins and some kind of flakes and a few little pieces of chocolate. I didn't even like to stop long enough to take a handful.

I stopped paddling then and waited for them to catch up to me. At least it gave me a chance to grab one of my granola bars. I ripped open the wrapper with my teeth and took a bite. I was so hungry that it actually tasted good. I stuffed it in my mouth, chewed, and swallowed it down. It wasn't long before they caught me.

"Do you see anything?" Jennie called out.

"Lots. Lots of water, lots of trees, lots of sky, and lots of rock. Lots and lots of nothing."

Their canoe glided in beside mine. My mother reached over and grabbed the side of my canoe, linking the two together.

"But you don't see the mouth of the river?" she asked.

"I wish."

"It should be around here someplace. Look."

She handed me the map—the same map we'd used to drive up through Quebec. I could see the little lake we were on. At one end was the little dot marked Waswanipi and at the opposite end of the lake was the entrance to the river. Following that little squiggly blue line, the Mattawa River would take us into Cashe Lake.

"It won't be much farther," my mother said. "Will it?"

I didn't know what to tell her. I looked at the map again.

I'd looked at this map dozens of times on the way up here, careful to make sure we made all the correct turns to get to Waswanipi. Now it was as though I was looking at it for the first time. This wasn't like driving. There were no signs, no gas stations or little stores, no one to help with directions. We weren't in Central Park or at some little holiday camp. We were by ourselves, on a lake in northern Quebec, in a couple of dinky little canoes, with nobody and nothing to guide us except for this map. And to make it even worse, it wasn't like once we got to Cashe Lake there'd be anybody there to help us. The camp was no more ... deserted.

From the first time my mother had mentioned this trip I'd been absolutely against the idea. I wanted nothing to do with urns and ashes and last wishes. I just wanted to stay with my friends in the city, and try hard to forget about all of that stuff. My father was dead. Scattering his ashes wasn't going to bring him back. It was just a big, stupid, bad idea. Just a dangerous waste of time, and my mother had dragged both me and Jennie along on it. Nice move, Mom. What now?

Maybe we could just forget the whole thing. Go back to that little village and get into our car and go home. That is, if we could find Waswanipi. If we couldn't even find the river, what guarantee was there that we'd be able to retrace our path back to the village?

"I think I see it," my sister said, pointing ahead. "Right over there."

I followed her arm, looking into the distance. All I saw was more bush.

"Yes, I think I see it too," Mom agreed. "See, where it looks as if the bush isn't as thick ... like there's a beach or a flat spot?"

"It's probably just a flat spot," I said.

"Maybe. Let's canoe toward that, anyway." They started paddling.

I was tired of looking over my shoulder and waiting for them to catch me, but that didn't mean I wanted them out in front of me, either. There was no way they were going to beat me there. Within a dozen strokes I'd caught them, and then I dug in deeper to pass by. I shifted the paddle from side to side, making sure the nose of the canoe stayed aimed at the right spot.

The closer I got, the less Jennie's spot looked like a river. But what it did look like was a flat spot where we could put the canoes in to shore. Judging by the increased grumbling in my stomach, it had to be pretty close to lunchtime. If the matches had dried out we could get something warm to eat. And maybe my mother and I could have a talk—a talk about going back. I understood why she wanted to do this—why she seemed to *need* to do this—but maybe it just wasn't meant to be. Or maybe we needed to try again later, with a tent that worked, and more supplies, and a bigger and better map.

Obviously, my mother hadn't thought this through. It was hard not to show how frustrated I was really feeling. I'd already bitten my tongue so many times it was raw.

I paddled closer to the spot. I was right—it was just a little beach. I paddled right up to the shore until the canoe hit bottom, then I took off my shoes and socks again, rolled up my pant legs, and jumped out. The freezing cold shot up my legs. It might have been summer, but this lake was as cold as ice. I waded to the bow of the canoe and dragged it up onto the shore.

The clothes draped over the top of my canoe were almost dry, so maybe the matches had dried out as well. I could just imagine a warm fire and a hot meal. As I walked ashore I looked past the thin row of shrubs and realized that I was standing on a little spit of land. Beyond that was ... the river! It curved out in one direction to meet the lake and in the other disappeared around a corner. We'd found it. *I'd* found it! First step completed! Maybe this wasn't the time to talk to my mother after all. Maybe we actually *could* do this thing!

"WAKE ME UP when it's time to go," my sister said. "I haven't felt this warm since we left home."

My sister and my mother were lying on a flat rock, baking in the warm midday sunshine. They had their own, dry clothes on again, so they were feeling and looking a lot more like themselves. I decided to let them rest for a minute while I cleaned up.

I rinsed out our bowls in the lake, using the dishcloth to wash away the last little crumbs of cereal—the cereal that had been our only food for three meals in a row now. The matches still wouldn't light. Mom said she thought they would, once they'd dried out completely. Seemed to me they were pretty dry already. If I was right, and the matches were permanently useless, then that meant we'd have no hot meals, or even a fire to warm us, for the whole trip. I hoped she was right. I *prayed* she was right.

Still, I was grateful for that cereal. And that said a lot more about my hunger than anything else. The cereal had at least filled my stomach and made me feel a little bit better. That, and the warm sun beaming down. And knowing exactly where we were on our little map. It felt good to be found.

"Let's get everything packed and get on our way," my mother said.

"Sounds good to me. If we really push ourselves we might even get to Cashe Lake before the end of today."

"That would be quite a push."

"But we have time. It's still only noon, and that gives us ten hours of light before we have to make camp, so why not?" I asked. "Besides, we're going with the river, with the current, so we should be able to make great time."

"We'll see. Let's just take it one step at a time."

I dropped the pot into the bow of my canoe along with all the other cooking utensils. I'd been carrying most of the supplies from the beginning, but now I moved almost everything else out of my mother's canoe and into mine. I left them with their sleeping bags, which were dry and lightweight. It was better if I took more of the heavy stuff. We could only move as fast the slowest canoe, so it was my way of speeding us up. I was still pretty angry about this whole trip, but the sooner we got there, the sooner we would get back. I *really* wanted to get back.

"Let me help you two get going," I offered.

We all pushed their canoe into the water and waded in after it. I steadied the canoe to allow first my sister and then my mother to climb in. Then I gave them a little push and they drifted out into open water. Next I pulled my canoe from shore, turned it around, and jumped in. They had gotten ahead of me, but it wouldn't be for long. I liked leading. I dug in deep, gaining on them with each stroke until I pulled even, and then pulled ahead.

As we rounded the little spit of land I felt the current start to pull me forward. This part of the trip was going to be a lot easier. Rather than fighting against the waves and wind on the open lake we were being helped along by the river. Of course, the easier it was going to be now, the harder it was going to be on the return trip, fighting against the current. But I'd worry about that later.

The river was fairly narrow, flat, and twisted and turned back and forth. There were trees and bushes pushing right down to the water's edge on one side. The other bank was higher—rocks rising up, dirt cliffs. There were hundreds of little birds— I guessed they were swallows—nesting in little holes in the cliffs. I'd expected to see a lot of wildlife, but other than a few seagulls in the distance this was the first I'd seen up close. They were frantically flying, swirling and circling, darting around. While I was fascinated by the swallows, they ignored me completely. They acted like I was an everyday sight, like a taxicab on Fifth Avenue. This was nothing like Fifth Avenue. This was nothing like New York. This was nothing like anything that I'd ever experienced before.

I couldn't get over the quiet. The only sound was my paddle slipping in and out of the water. But then, why shouldn't it be quiet? It wasn't just that there were no cabs, no buildings, no offices, no airplanes—there were no *people*. Wow ... no people. There was probably nobody between here and that dinky little town across the lake. Just me and my mother and Jennie.

I looked over my shoulder, back down the river. They weren't there. They hadn't made it around the last bend in the river yet. I was completely alone.

I suddenly *felt* all alone. I knew in my head they were just around the bend, that they'd appear in a few seconds, but I felt a growing sense of panic. *Maybe I should paddle back, or ...* But just as I thought that, the bright red tip of the canoe appeared and they came into view. The bad feelings just drained away.

I started paddling again. I was actually beginning to enjoy this. It reminded me more of our little canoe trips at camp. There was also a feeling of progress. Here, close to the shore, helped along by the current, I felt like I was moving really quickly— no ... it didn't just *feel* like I was moving faster ... I really *was*.

I pulled my paddle out of the water. The current was picking up. The river was racing. Even though I'd stopped paddling, my canoe was moving faster and faster. The banks on each side were getting steeper, rising up into tall cliffs. The river was also getting narrower, which meant the same volume of water was being forced into a smaller passage. That explained it. There wasn't any other reason ...

And then I heard something ... like the sound of rushing wind, or a crowd in the distance getting closer. But it was neither.

But it was neither. It was the sound of rushing water.

CHAPTER FIVE

UP AHEAD THE RIVER NARROWED, and the water was white and rolling and bumpy, boiling over jagged rocks—rapids! Panicked, I looked from side to side to find a place to get out of the stream, but the banks were already too steep and seemed to rise even higher just ahead. I dug in with my paddle and tried to steer off toward the side to try to find something—a handhold, a tree, anything that I could grab on to. As I made my cut I saw my sister and mother upstream. I had to warn them! They had to get out of the river—now!

"Rapids! Rapids! Get out!" I screamed.

I couldn't tell if they'd heard me, but they'd definitely seen me. They stopped paddling. That wouldn't help them. They needed to paddle … paddle to the riverbank and get out.

"Rapids! Danger! Get out!" I screamed again. I waved my paddle over my head, trying desperately to warn them.

Maybe they understood, or maybe they saw the rapids up ahead, because they started to move quickly now, digging in with their own paddles, cutting toward the shore. They were going to make it! My canoe smacked up against something and I was jolted out of my thoughts as freezing cold water splashed into my face. The rapids weren't up ahead anymore— I was right in the middle of them now! There was no hope of getting out. I had to get through them.

The canoe dropped out from under me. For a split second I thought I was going to be thrown. I hooked my heels under the seat to hold me in place, but that didn't stop my stomach from flying up and into my throat. The canoe bucked and rocked as it hit another drop. Up ahead there were lethal-looking rocks sticking out of the water and whitewater foaming over and around them. I had to steer past them. I dug in with my paddle on the right—I couldn't fight the current, but I could still try to steer. The canoe shot off to the right, but not quite far enough. The tip of the canoe bashed into the rocks, and I was jolted over violently. Then the canoe tipped forward and dropped down. I almost lost my leg-lock on the canoe and my grip on the paddle, but somehow I stayed attached to both.

There was no time to feel scared or relieved—there were more rocks, more drops, straight ahead.

I swung the paddle over to the other side of the canoe. There were rocks to the right and open water on the left side. I leaned hard into the paddle, sinking the whole blade into the water.

"Come on, come on, move!" I yelled at the canoe.

It was as if it had heard me. It cut sharply across the face of the rocks, moving almost directly across the river. And then the current grabbed me again and I shot through the opening and rolled down the funnel of water that was racing around the rocks. I quickly picked up speed as I went over a series of little bumps and drops. All I could do was hold on and hope. I was going faster and faster.

A gigantic outcrop of rock rose up in the middle of the river, breaking it into two streams. Right or left? Which was better, which way should I go? Before I could even try to decide, the decision was made for me. I shot off to the left. I dropped down— at least three feet or more—and the bow of the canoe dipped beneath the surface as water splashed up and over top of me, soaking me and spilling into the canoe. I let go of the paddle and grabbed on to the canoe, desperately trying to stay anchored in it. It dropped again, and the whole world seemed to flip over as I was tossed into the air. I tried to scream out, but before any words could escape I slammed into the water and disappeared beneath the surface!

I clawed at the water, scrambling to get back to the surface, but I was dragged farther down, tossed, turned around, spun like a sock in a washing machine. I was powerless to fight it. I could see the light, see the surface, but I couldn't get to it. I realized that right there, right then, I was going to drown. I was going to die. I stopped struggling—and suddenly I popped to the surface.

I gasped for air as my arms worked to keep my head above the water. My life jacket helped—I could hardly believe it hadn't been ripped right off me. I was facing backwards, back up the river. I tried to turn myself around and then I smashed against something and I cried out in pain. The force of the blow spun me around again. Now I was facing forward and I could see what was ahead—more rocks, more whitewater, stretching out farther than I could see.

I started to scream again. But what was the point? There was nobody who could hear or help. I clapped my mouth shut before water could rush in, and I dropped down another fall and slipped beneath the surface once more. I popped back up and immediately hit another drop, and then another and another. I tried to gulp down a mouthful of air but water surged into my mouth and down my throat. I spat it back out, and then I smashed into something, and a searing pain raced down my side. I grabbed at the rocks, digging in with my fingertips, trying desperately to hold on, fighting against the river, which was dragging me farther down. I threw one arm over the rock and then looped the second over. I fought against the current that tried to rip me free ... how long could I hold on before—

"Give me your hand!"

I looked up. There was a man standing on a rocky ledge, leaning out, trying to reach me. This couldn't be real ... it was a dream or—

"Give me your hand!" he screamed again.

I took one hand from the rock and reached out for him. But I couldn't hold on with only one hand, and the current captured me, ripped me off the rock. And then he grabbed me, his hand locked around my wrist. I hung there, in the river, not moving, the water pounding down on me, pummelling my head and face, caught. At last he hauled me out, and I practically flew through the air, landing on top of him, on top of the rocky outcrop.

"Is there anybody else with you?" he yelled over the roar of the water.

"I was alone ... in the canoe ..."

"Speak up!" he yelled.

"My mother and sister ... they were behind me ... in another canoe ... I think they got out of the river ... before the rapids."

"You think?" he demanded. "Did they or didn't they?" His voice was calm but his bright blue eyes were sharp and piercing.

"I ... I don't know ... I tried to warn them but the rapids got me before I could see if they were safe."

He released his grip on my wrist and jumped to his feet. He rushed back to the protruding rock and stood there, poised, waiting, arms outstretched, eyes searching upriver. He looked like a cat—an old cat, poised to pounce. He was an old man with a scraggly beard and thinning hair—not tall, slight of build, but he had to be strong the way he'd pulled me from the river. I could still feel where his fingers had dug into my wrist to hold me.

I rolled over to my knees and staggered to my feet. If the others had gone into the rapids they'd have to come this way. All we could do was watch and hope they were already safe. I lurched over to his side, getting as close to the edge of the rocks as I dared.

"What were they wearing?" he asked.

"Um ... sandals and shorts, I think."

"Did they both have life jackets, like you? What colour?"

"My sister for sure ... but I don't know about my mother ... I think maybe ... red ... like mine ... the life jackets are red."

"Look for red, look for dark, look for anything under the surface of the water. There are just the two of them, correct? No one else?"

"There were just the three of us."

"You should never have tried to go through those rapids."

"I wasn't *trying* to go through. I didn't know——" I stopped. I thought I'd heard something over the roar of the river. Then I saw a flash of red, no, two flashes of red. My mother and sister were running down the opposite shore, screaming, yelling out.

"I'm here! I'm here!" I screamed.

They stopped running. They waved, and my mother threw an arm around Jennie, who then buried her face in Mom's side. My mother yelled out something, but the roar of the river drowned out her words.

"Are you hurt? Are you able to walk?" the man asked.

"Both. I'm hurt, but I can walk."

"Come," the man said. "There's a place to cross just down from here." He motioned for my mother and sister to go downstream as well, and they started walking on the other shore, paralleling us.

I trailed after him. He was moving quickly, jumping from rock to rock. My legs felt weak and rubbery
and I felt unsure on my feet. I struggled to keep up
with him. He was dressed in a buckskin jacket, and
I wondered if he was a trapper or something.

He turned around. "Maybe you should sit."

"I'm fine ... I'm just not fast. Is it much farther?"

He shook his head. "Just below the waterfall."

"Waterfall ... there's a waterfall?"

"Not a big one. Three or four metres."

"A metre ... is that like a yard?"

"You must be an American," he said, and smirked.
"About the same. Come."

He followed a path that led away from the river.
I hesitated for a second and looked across the river,
trying to see my mother and sister. I couldn't. They
must have moved away from the river as well.

I lurched down the path. It cut off sharply to the
side and then dropped down. The rocks were almost
like steps, and I climbed carefully down, moving
slowly. The old man was standing at the bottom of the
rocks, waiting, watching, maybe ready to reach out to
help if I fell or stumbled. I didn't need his help, and
he didn't offer.

I followed as we continued around rocks and trees
and bushes. The path cut again, this time back toward
the river. The ground levelled and we came out to a

small, sandy beach. There was a large pool of water that caught the river as it crashed over a waterfall ... a *waterfall!* I stopped and stared at it. I'd almost gone over that. If he hadn't grabbed me and pulled me out of the river when he did, I would have gone over for sure.

"Your mother," he said, pointing across the river.

Mom and Jennie were standing in a little clearing on the other side of the river, on the other side of the wide pool. They saw us and waved, and I waved back. I was so happy to see them. *So* happy.

The old man walked over to the edge of the pool and waded into the water. I knew he expected me to follow. I hesitated at the water's edge. I was reluctant ... anxious ... scared to get back into the water.

"Come," he said. "There is no cause for concern."

I had no choice but to follow. The bottom was soft and the slope gentle. At the halfway mark, the water was just over my waist. We kept moving, and passed the deepest spot, and soon the water got shallower and shallower.

My mother and sister waded in to greet me. They both threw their arms around me, and my sister was crying—*of course* my sister was crying.

"It's all right. I'm okay," I said. I felt like crying too, but I couldn't do that, especially not in front of some stranger.

"We were so scared. You must have been *so scared*!" Jennie said.

"He was very brave," the man told her.

My mother was shaking. "I was so worried. I was terrified that … that …"

"You were right to be worried, but he's quite all right."

"We were so shocked to see somebody else here," my mother said.

"As was I."

"We're so lucky you were nearby!"

He shrugged. "Not luck. Fate. We are often placed where we are needed."

"He pulled me out," I said. "I would have gone over the waterfall without him."

"I was there to offer him a hand," he said.

"He pulled me right out of the river!"

"He was very calm, very capable," the man said. "And no sooner was he out than he was concerned about your safety."

"Thank you so much for your help. But where are my manners? This is my daughter, Jennie."

He bowed slightly from the waist.

"And of course you've met Brian."

"But not by name." He offered his hand and we shook.

"And I'm Catherine … Cathy Martin."

"My pleasure." Again he bowed in her direction. "And I am Pierre."

"Pierre …?"

"Just Pierre. It is my pleasure to meet you all."

The way he spoke was different. I knew that people in different places had different accents, and I also knew that lots of people up here spoke French, but it wasn't just that he was speaking English with a French accent. It was more like there was *no* accent. His words were very precise, planned, as though he knew what he was going to say and he wasn't going to waste any extra words saying it.

"But I must admit that my pleasure is mixed with surprise." He furrowed his brow. "Brian has explained that he was not trying to go through the rapids, that he simply did not know they were there."

"They weren't marked on our map," my mother said.

Now he looked shocked. "Are you sure?"

"Positive," my mother said. "I've got it right here."

She pulled the map out of her pocket, unfolded it partway, and handed it to him.

He looked at the map, then at my mother, and finally at me. His eyes were wide open. Now he looked shocked *and* surprised.

"This … this … map," he said, pointing at it. "It's a *road* map."

"Yes, we got it from the information centre at the border when we entered Canada. We used it to get up to Waswanipi," my mother explained.

"But you don't have any other maps?" He no longer sounded calm. Now he sounded angry. "No maps showing the rivers and lakes?"

"They're on the map. See?" she said, pointing. "There's the lake we're on now, and we're heading to Cashe Lake ... it's right ... right *there*."

He shook his head. "And you have no other maps? You are on a canoe trip with only a road map?"

"Yes. I thought that—"

"No, *madame*, you did not think at all. Only the most experienced traveller, completely familiar with the route, would even dream of attempting this kind of trip without the proper maps and charts! Do you have the necessary experience?" he demanded angrily.

"My husband was the expert on camping and canoeing."

"Your husband? He is obviously not as expert as you suggest if he would allow his family to take such a trip! What was he thinking, to endanger his wife and children in such a thoroughly hazardous and foolhardy—?"

"Our father is dead!" I snapped.

His mouth opened and his expression changed to shock. The only person more surprised than him was me. I couldn't believe I'd just blurted that out.

"That's why we're here," my mother said. "That's why we've come up here ... to scatter his ashes."

"Oh—oh my gosh," I stammered. "The ashes ... they were in my canoe!" I didn't know where they were because I didn't even know where my canoe was. I felt as if I'd been kicked in the stomach.

"It's okay, Brian," my mother said. She tried to wrap her arm around me but I backed away.

"No, it's not. They're gone, and it's my fault."

"You had no control over the river," the man said. "You are blameless. But perhaps you are worrying unnecessarily."

I shook my head. "They're gone ... lost."

"What is lost may be found. I will search the river. I want you three to go back to my camp. It is just by the place where I helped you from the river."

"No, I'll help you look."

"No," he said. "You need to rest."

"I'm fine."

"You are not fine. Besides, you have to lead your sister and mother to my camp. Only you know where you were pulled from the water." He paused. "Please, have faith. If it can be found, I will find it."

What he was saying made sense, but I still wanted to be part of the search—it was my father, and it was my fault.

"There is a pot of coffee warming on the fire," he said. "Go ... you could probably use something to warm you."

Reluctantly, I agreed.

CHAPTER SIX

PIERRE'S CAMP was on a rocky point overlooking the rapids, with bush behind. It was pretty simple but well organized. The fire was on a large rock, with smaller rocks forming a wall to keep it in place. He had a simple, old backpack hanging from a tree, a few supplies, a pot, a frying pan, some cooking utensils, and a beat-up old sleeping bag that looked older than he was. There was no tent. Either it was in his pack or he didn't have one. Maybe he was sleeping under his canoe, the way I had the night before. That would explain why he'd brought it to his camp instead of leaving it down by the river. Then I thought about it a bit more and figured that he'd probably walked his stuff here, to avoid the rapids. He must have been in the middle of a portage, and he'd decided to stop here and rest for the night. He was pretty old, after all.

"Do you think he'll find it?" Jennie asked.

"I have faith in him," Mom said. "You always have to look on the bright side."

Not always, I thought, but I didn't bother to say that. "If he doesn't find the urn, there's no point in going on," I said.

"I think the trip is over, regardless," my mother agreed.

I gave her a questioning look.

"Pierre was right. We're not prepared."

"He was rude!" I muttered. It was one thing for *me* to criticize my mother, but he didn't have that right. She'd been through a lot, and she didn't need to take garbage from some stranger

"Maybe he was very … direct, but what he said was true. We didn't bring proper maps, and now at least half of our supplies are gone. "

"And we don't even have any matches that light," Jennie said, glumly.

"Besides, after what happened to Brian … what might have happened … we have to go back."

Part of me was incredibly relieved. I hadn't wanted to be on this trip in the first place, I'd told her from the beginning it was a bad idea, and I was more than ready to go home. But another part of me wanted to argue with my mother, to tell her that we had to go on and finish what we'd started.

Maybe it was because I knew she'd never stop thinking about it and talking about it until we did what
we'd set out to do at Cashe Lake. And maybe it was
still bugging me, the way the old guy had made me
feel, like we had no idea what we were doing and
had no business being here. Still, the biggest part of
me knew she was right. We didn't have the right
equipment or enough supplies, and we had absolutely no idea what was still ahead of us. If we
hadn't known about this set of rapids, what else
didn't we know about?

My mother looked defeated, but I knew she was
thinking hard, trying to find some way to make it
all right.

"Besides," she said, "even if we can't find the ashes,
we have sort of done what your father wanted. He
canoed in these waters, too. He'd have had to pass this
way to get to Cashe."

"And doesn't the water here flow into Cashe
Lake?" Jennie asked.

"Yes," my mother agreed. "So, in a way, the ashes
will get to Cashe Lake ... eventually."

I knew what she was trying to do—make us feel
better, make herself feel better. It was the truth,
as well as a rationalization. It didn't matter. It was
over. We were heading back, and that was all that
really counted.

"Hopefully, Pierre can at least find the canoe," my mother said.

I'd been thinking so much about what was in the canoe that I hadn't even thought about the canoe itself. I wondered what shape it would be in if he did find it. We'd smashed into a whole lot of rocks, that canoe and I, on our wild ride. I reached down and touched my sore side and recoiled slightly from the touch.

"Even if he can't find the other canoe, I think the three of us can fit in one, now that we aren't carrying so many supplies," she said. "It will be okay ... won't it?"

Before I could answer, Pierre silently walked into camp. Slung over one shoulder was my pack. And then he held it up—the blue-grey metal urn holding my father's ashes!

"You found them!" I practically yelled, jumping to my feet. I rushed over and took both the urn and my pack. "Thanks."

He smiled and nodded.

The urn had a dent but it was still intact. The pack was heavy—soaked through and through—but the straps were still done up. Whatever had been in there was still in there, including my very wet CD player. So much for music for the rest of this trip.

"I found them just downriver. Along with the canoe."

"The canoe—that's great!" Mom said.

"Not so great. One side is bashed in very badly. I'm afraid it's beyond repair and cannot be used."

"That's awful," I said.

He shrugged. "It is simply a canoe. It might just as easily have been your head. How are you feeling?"

"My side is sore."

"Come, let me look."

I lifted up my shirt.

"Where does it hurt?" he asked.

I thought that was probably a good sign. It obviously didn't look too bad.

"Right there," I said, touching the spot.

He put pressure there and I jumped and yelped, trying not to do either.

"Hold still," he ordered. He ran his fingers along my ribs. There was only that one spot.

"Nothing's broken, but you will feel some discomfort, especially when you paddle."

I pulled my shirt back down. "We're not going to do much of that now," I said.

"We're going back," my mother explained. "I guess we'll all have to share the one canoe."

"Is it a big canoe?" Pierre asked.

"The same size as the smashed one," I said. "But we're not going far, just back to Waswanipi, where we started."

"And you wanted to take the ashes to Cashe. It has a special meaning ... yes?" Pierre asked.

"Yes," my mother said. "My husband grew up in Montreal and he spent his summers up at a camp on Cashe. He never forgot how happy he was there. It's what he wanted."

"But, you ... you three are not from Montreal ... somewhere around New York."

"Yes! We live right in Manhattan," my mother said. "You could tell by the accents, right?"

"Yes. Fairly distinctive. But your husband was Canadian."

"He became an American," I said. "Like us."

"Actually, he had dual citizenship, as do both my children."

"I'm an *American*," I said.

"You are American *and* Canadian," she insisted.

"It is possible to be both," Pierre said.

"I hope we can come back to Canada one day to finish what we started," my mother said. "I hope we can try the trip again, I really do. But next time we'll have better equipment and maps, and perhaps a guide."

"I would be pleased to offer my services," Pierre said.

"You're a guide?" she asked.

"Not by profession, but I am familiar with these waters. I have been travelling this area since I was Brian's age."

"We don't need your help," I snapped. "We can get along fine."

"Really?" he asked, although it wasn't actually a question.

"Really."

He shrugged. "Whether it is back to Waswanipi or forward to Cashe, I am at your service. Regardless of your choice, in all good conscience, I cannot leave you here alone."

"We'll be fine if we go back to Waswanipi. We know the route now, and it isn't that far," I said.

"Then I will accompany you there."

"Are you heading in that direction?" she asked.

He shook his head. "I was moving downstream myself."

"We really don't want to inconvenience you. That would take you two days out of your way."

"I have no agenda, or timetable, or set destination, as it happens. I am here entirely for the pleasure of the journey, and I am now at your service."

My mother didn't answer right away, which meant she was thinking about his offer.

"I understand that you might be feeling discouraged and ready to return home. But if you should change your mind, I would consider it an honour to accompany your family to help you complete this trip. What you are doing … it is … it is the *right* thing to do."

My mother smiled. "Then I think we'll accept your offer. We'll go forward."

WE MOVED PIERRE'S CANOE and equipment down the path past the waterfall and waded across the river. His canoe was nothing like our fibreglass rentals. His was wooden, made of cedar strips all glued together, varnished and shiny and with a dark red canvas. On the side hand painted in white letters it said, *Ça Ira*. Was that somebody's name or something? Did this canoe belong to some guy named Ira? I didn't know much about canoes, but I knew this one was expensive. It looked more like a work of art than a real canoe.

We left my mother and sister to set up camp while we walked back up the river to bring down their canoe and supplies. There was a path, but it was rough, rocky, and uphill all the way. I was surprised by how quickly Pierre moved. He was no spring chicken. He had to be in his seventies. His buckskin jacket looked at least that old. I was curious how old he really was, but it wasn't the sort of question you could just ask somebody. Old or not, I was working hard just to keep up with him. Maybe he wasn't getting tired, but I was getting winded.

"You know this river pretty well," I said, trying to make conversation.

"Yes, I have been through this passage many times," he said. "I have even taken the first two parts of the rapids by canoe."

"On purpose?" I asked.

He laughed, stopped, and turned around. "I have been through rapids that are larger and longer. Perhaps when we find your mother's canoe we will take the river back."

"The river ... through the rapids?"

He winked. "Not this time."

He started back up the trail. For that split second before I knew he was kidding I had felt a rush of fear. As far as I was concerned, I was content to walk the rest of this whole trip.

"This is certainly different from New York City," he said over his shoulder.

"You can't get any more different," I agreed.

"Wonderful city, New York."

"You've been there?"

"Many, many times."

"It's the best city in the world!"

"What do you think of Paris?"

"Um ... I hear it's very nice."

"You have never been there?"

"No."

"I also think London, Hong Kong, and Tokyo might compete for the title of 'world's best city.'"

"I haven't been to those, either," I admitted.

"And we mustn't overlook Beijing, Moscow, Rome, and perhaps Vienna."

"You've been to all of those places?"

"Those and hundreds of places in between. Travel offers a tremendous opportunity for education. As I discovered the world, I discovered myself."

I almost laughed out loud. Did he get that off a bumper sticker or from a fortune cookie in a Chinese restaurant?

"It wasn't until my father took our family to Europe when I was just a little younger than you, twelve, that I discovered my love of travelling."

"Travelling is okay, but I like being home."

"There is no place like home, and New York is certainly an exciting place to live. Museums, art galleries, the opera, ballet."

"Not to mention the Mets, Rangers, and Knicks."

"I am familiar with the Mets. My father was most interested in baseball. And of course, I know the New York Rangers. But I am unfamiliar with the Knicks. They are a sports team of some kind?"

"You don't know the New York Knicks, the basketball team?" I questioned in amazement.

"I do not know the team, but I am familiar with the game. It was in fact invented by a Canadian."

"No way!" I protested. "James Naismith invented basketball."

"And he was a Canadian. But as I say, I do not follow basketball."

"So you're a hockey fan."

"Not really."

"But I thought all Canadians were hockey crazy."

"Not all. I prefer skiing and canoeing. Speaking of which, there is your mother's canoe."

Jennie and my mother had dragged the canoe partway up onto the shore before running off to look for me, but they'd left the tail end still partially in the water, bouncing in the current. It looked as though it might be pulled back into the water any minute.

The spot where they had made it to shore looked to be one of the last places where they could have gotten out of the river before the rapids. I felt a sudden rush of fear. It was terrible to think about anything bad happening to Jennie or my mother. I couldn't afford to let that happen.

"It looks as though you warned them just in time," Pierre said.

"I guess so."

He pulled the canoe completely free of the water. Both of their packs were in the bottom, along with their sleeping bags.

"This gear is not tied down in any way. It was just tossed into the canoe." There was disgust on his face and in his voice.

"They tipped their canoe yesterday and things were put out to dry," I said, trying to make an excuse.

"If we are to make this portage in one trip, we will need to organize things."

"One trip? There's no way we can do that. There's too much stuff," I protested.

"It can be done if we organize the equipment. I can take one of the packs and the canoe."

"I don't know, the canoe is pretty heavy. It took both of us to carry your canoe down."

"There were two of us, so two carried it. I can manage it on my own. And this canoe is lighter, made of fibreglass."

I had no choice but to believe him. He'd obviously portaged on his own already, but it couldn't have been easy. "How many trips did it take for you to move your things down to the spot where you're camped?"

"One."

"Wait, you carried all your gear and your canoe in one trip?" I asked, doubt dripping from my voice.

"I carried nothing. The river carried me."

"You came down the river, over the rapids?" I asked. Was he joking or bragging?

"I told you, I have taken these rapids before. With practice, a skilled canoeist can run the smaller rapids."

"These are small?"

"Compared to some. I stopped just before the waterfall—that is not passable, although you were close to making an attempt on your own."

"I could have gotten out by myself," I grumbled.

He cocked his head to the side as though he was studying me. "Perhaps."

"No, really, I was just getting ready to pull myself out when you grabbed me."

"In that case, would you like to change your mind and try canoeing partway down right now?"

My eyes opened and I took a half-step back.

He smiled and chuckled to himself. "You will need to get back on the river, Brian—back on the horse that threw you—but not now, not today. Today, we will portage around the rapids."

CHAPTER SEVEN

I HEARD A SOUND and jerked awake, my heart pounding a mile a minute. I listened intently and tried to see. I wondered what time it was. It was still dark, but not as dark as it had been. We had to be getting close to morning.

It seemed as if I'd woken up a hundred times through the night, reacting to every little noise. I snuggled down into my sleeping bag now, safely cocooned in the nylon and stuffing. Not exactly what I'd need to protect me from a bear or a badger or a wolf, but it did feel warm and safe. I might not have been so nervous if I'd been sleeping in a tent, but this was my second night huddled under an overturned canoe. Pierre had done the same with his canoe, and my mother and sister had used the tent.

Pierre had cut up some branches and they were using them as poles. He'd said something about how it was "better to be ingenious than a genius" when camping. It certainly hadn't taken a genius to cut a few branches, and I could have done the same thing if we hadn't lost our hatchet. The poles weren't perfect, but the tent was almost standing up. Maybe it was time to join my family in the tent. Yeah, right, like another layer of thin nylon would block out the sounds or the dangers.

I shifted around in my sleeping bag, trying to find the best spot to get comfortable. But even at home, in my own bed, I hadn't been sleeping very well, so it wasn't likely that the hard ground was going to send me off to dreamland. And to make it worse, all night my mind had been replaying my trip through the rapids. It was as though everything had happened so fast that I hadn't been able to think about it at the time, not even to be afraid. But now, lying in the dark, with nothing to do but think, my brain was running through it over and over again. That was probably the scariest experience of my life. I'd nearly died. And every time I shifted in my sleep, the pain in my side reminded me. It was awfully sore.

I caught sight of a shadowy figure and recognized who it was and what he was doing. Pierre was crouched over the firepit, stacking kindling. He was going to start the fire. There was a small flare of light—a match—and then a glow, and then the fire began to blaze. I could just make out Pierre and some faint images beyond him. There was a hint of the sun starting to brighten the sky. I guessed it was time to get up.

I undid the sleeping-bag zipper and Pierre turned at the sound.

"Good morning," I said.

"Good morning." He warmed his hands over the growing fire. "Sleep well?"

"Not great. There are so many sounds out here."

"As opposed to the silence of Manhattan?"

"It's different sounds. Traffic and sirens are like lullabies to me."

"The sounds of wind and water and night animals are the same for me," Pierre said.

I stood up and started to stretch but yelped in pain.

"Your ribs are hurting?" he asked.

"A little. What time is it?"

"I would think about five-thirty."

"Do you always get up this early?" I asked.

"Hardly ever, but today we have a long way to go," he said.

"What's the plan?"

"We eat, pack, and start down the river."

"And we're past the rapids, right?" I asked anxiously.

"Yes, the rapids are behind us. There are only a few … ripples."

"What's a 'ripple'?" The only ripples I knew about were in Ruffles potato chips.

"A ripple ... a small, almost unnoticeable drop ... a little ripple," he said, making a slight waving motion with his hand.

"Could we portage around them?"

"That is not necessary."

"But *could* we?"

"We could walk all the way to the lake if we chose to."

"How much longer would that take?"

"Two, perhaps three days."

I didn't like that either. There was no way I wanted to be carrying our canoes when they could be carrying us.

"Brian, I understand your hesitancy. But you have to have faith. I know this river, and I know this can be done. We will get safely to Cashe."

I didn't answer.

"If at any time during this trip you feel we need to put in to shore, I will respect that. Okay?"

I nodded. "Okay. But won't you be sharing a canoe with my sister?"

"I believe it would be wise for you and me to share a canoe."

"But Jennie's the weakest, so she needs the most help."

"Right now, you are the most in need of help. Are your ribs very sore?"

"I can paddle," I said, defiantly.

"That was not the question."

I didn't want to acknowledge it, but he'd heard the yelp. "Yeah, they hurt."

"Perhaps tomorrow or the next day you will feel better, but until then, you will be more passenger than paddler."

"But I'm fine … really!"

"Raise your arms above your head," he said.

Slowly I raised my arms, stopping when I grimaced in pain.

"It would be better if, at least today, you did not paddle much … perhaps a stroke or two to help me along, but that's all. And I think your sister would prefer to be in a canoe with your mother. Unlike you, she needs your mother's presence and comfort."

I wanted to argue, but I knew he was right on both counts.

"Enough discussion." He held up a pot. "Fill this with water so we can put it on to boil."

PIERRE STEADIED our remaining rented canoe as my mother and sister carefully climbed in. Their gear was all meticulously stowed in there, held in place with rope and bungee cords. He held the stern of their canoe, easing them into the river. Then we pulled his cedar-strip craft off the shore until it was afloat.

"Here," Pierre said. He handed me a paddle. "Very strong." It felt warm in my hand.

My paddle had gone over the falls with everything else, and we hadn't been able to find it. My rental paddle was plastic and metal. This one was wooden.

"It is hand-carved, crafted by the same man who made my canoe. A paddle must be just right," Pierre said. "It is for the canoeist an essential tool, like a hammer for a carpenter or a wrench for a mechanic."

"I was thinking we'd just be canoeing today and not fixing a car or building a shelf."

"Ah … the beauty is that all are very similar if done well. Now, climb in," Pierre said. "But today, you will mainly hold the paddle, and I will be doing the work."

Carefully I climbed in. He pushed the canoe forward and nimbly jumped in as it surged forward.

My mother and sister were well ahead of us on the river, but we quickly closed the gap until we were right beside them. We all knew that Pierre's canoe would be the leader. A few more powerful strokes and we were in front.

I just held my paddle. I hadn't even dipped it into the water yet. But I wanted to be more than just luggage. Tentatively, I dipped the paddle into the water. I felt my side ache with the pressure. I had to ease off, but I was still going to try to help.

"I was wondering," I said, "how long have you been out here?"

"Almost two weeks," Pierre said.

"That's a long time to be by yourself."

"I enjoy the solitude."

"I guess we ruined that."

"Not ruined. Changed. Things happen for a reason."

Not everything, I thought to myself.

"I think the longest I've ever been alone was a couple of hours," I told him.

"There is something about a canoe trip that makes it different from any other experience. Out here, stripped of all worldly goods and concerns, a man is able to think clearly."

"You must have done a lot of thinking in two weeks," I said.

He didn't answer, so I knew not to ask him what he was thinking about. Better to stick to simple things.

"The letters on the side of your canoe," I said. "That's French, right?"

"Yes."

"What does it mean?"

"Roughly translated it means *it will go—this canoe will get there*."

That was reassuring. I hoped our journey would be fine. I hoped that we'd get there.

"How long before we get to Cache Lake?"

"Not far. Perhaps two hours at this pace."

"I was hoping it would be shorter. The longer we go with the river, the longer we're going to have to fight upstream on the return trip."

"We won't need to make a return trip."

I spun around to look at him. What did he mean by that?

"But we have to go back to get our car!"

"Yes, but I suggest to you that it might be wiser to continue to travel with the flow of the water. We can continue on from Cashe Lake, down a river called Nappawee, to another village I know. It's not much more than a few houses on a lumber trail, it doesn't even have a name, but from there we can arrange to have someone drive us back to your car. It will be better to let the water carry us than to fight the current."

"I guess that makes sense. Going with the flow is a lot easier."

"Of course, that does not mean that it is always the correct course. Sometimes you have no choice but to go against the current." He chuckled under his breath. "Many people believe that I have done that even when there was no need."

I had no idea what he meant by that.

"Can you show me that village?"

"Show you? I will take you."

"I mean on a map … one of those canoe maps you told us about."

"I do not have any maps with me."

"But you told us we were supposed to have one of those!"

"You *should* have had one. It was reckless and dangerous to try this trip without a proper map."

"But *you* don't have one?"

"Do you need a map to find your way from your bedroom to the kitchen?" he asked.

"Of course not."

"This is *my* home. I know this river, I know these lakes. It is different for me."

"Isn't it just as dangerous to be out here by yourself?" I asked. "Aren't you supposed to always travel with somebody?" I was thinking about how we'd been taught at camp to always use the buddy system when we were swimming.

"It is always better to travel as one wise man than in a company of fools," I heard him say.

Was he calling us fools? Should I say something? What was the point? We *had* been idiots.

We travelled along in silence for a while. He seemed really comfortable with silence. Me, I liked words.

"Were you born up here?"

"I was born in Montreal."

"Like my father."

"And like your father, I found that my time here, away from the city, offered me many of my finest moments. There is something about a canoeing expedition that purifies you." He paused. "I would imagine that going through the rapids *without* a canoe might be both purifying *and* cleansing ... no?"

Was he taking another shot at me? I spun around. He was smiling. I was just about to say something when the canoe bucked and dropped slightly. My stomach lurched upward into my throat.

"Here are some of those ripples."

I spun back around. There were little whitecaps, but nothing like anything I'd experienced the day before.

"Do you want me to put to shore?" he asked, keeping his word.

I shook my head. "Just go." I grabbed firmly onto both sides of the canoe and braced myself. I could do this.

We hit another little dip and I hooked my legs under the seat. There was no way I was leaving this canoe. We hit another little dip, and then another ... and then the water just flattened out. It was flat and blue. That couldn't be it, could it?

I turned back around to face Pierre. "That's it?"

"Just ripples."

And I discovered something new: rapids were scary, but ripples? Ripples I could handle.

CHAPTER EIGHT

THERE WAS A CHILL in the air. It was amazing to me how quickly it could go from too hot during the day to too cold when the sun set. In the city, the concrete and cement always held some of the warmth of the day. Here and now, the fire was our only source of heat, and it felt good.

Along with the heat came light—a little arc of light that spread out across our campsite. Beyond that was complete darkness. There had to be a million stars in the sky but they failed to add any light, and the moon was low and lost behind the trees.

Pierre had guided us to a good spot he knew for setting up camp. You could see where someone else before us had made a fire on the rocks. It was kind of comforting to know that even though we were alone, we weren't the first people to have ever passed this way.

Jennie poked at the fire with a stick, kicking up ashes and sparks, which floated up into the night sky before disappearing.

"So, Pierre, Brian tells me that you're originally from Montreal, like my husband," my mother said.

"Yes, Montreal is where I was born, and where I now live."

"Oh, I assumed you lived up here," she said.

"No. This is not where I live, although it is the place where I feel most alive. Montreal is a big city. Do you know what part your husband was from?"

"Point St. Charles."

"I know the district. Tough area."

"My father said the same thing," I said.

"May I ask how he made his way from Montreal to New York?"

"Hockey."

"He skated to New York?" Pierre asked. There was laughter in his eyes.

"Practically," my mother said. "He came down to attend college on a hockey scholarship. That's where we met."

"You were on a hockey scholarship too?"

Jennie and I both laughed. Obviously, if he'd ever seen my mother on skates, he would have known just how funny his joke was.

"I was there getting my degree. We met, fell in love, and got married right after we graduated."

"And the two of you decided to stay in the United States," Pierre said.

"That was a hard decision. Ben—my husband—his parents died a few years after we graduated. He didn't have any brothers or sisters or, really, any close family, so we just stayed in New York. But I have to tell you, he always loved to come back to Canada. He followed the news, and when the Olympics were on we always knew which country he'd be cheering for."

"And which country *I'd* be cheering for," I said. "And we both knew which country was going to win the most medals!"

"The United States is a giant in such things," Pierre said.

"U.S.A. all the way," I said. "I'm proud of my country."

He gave me a questioning look. "I thought you had citizenship in *two* countries."

"Maybe, but I'm all American."

"Such pride and patriotism is a wonderful thing. Doubtless, the United States is the greatest industrial giant that ever existed."

"And the strongest," I added.

"Certainly a very powerful nation. Did your family come to Canada often to visit?"

"Hardly ever," my mother said. "Between our jobs and school and commitments in the community there just never seemed to be time."

"I'm sorry to hear that."

"Brian tells me that you have travelled around the world," she said.

I had told her a lot about what we'd talked about, and now I was feeling embarrassed, like I'd been caught doing something I shouldn't have done, like I'd been gossiping about him.

"I have had that pleasure."

"Was your travelling for business or pleasure?" she asked.

"Both."

"My husband travelled a lot on business. What line of work were you in?" she asked.

He didn't answer right away. "You could say that I worked for the government."

"Like a civil servant?" I asked.

"Yes, something very much like that. I often travelled for diplomatic purposes."

"That must have been very exciting!"

"Often not nearly as exciting as one might expect," he said.

"My husband used to say that every room in every Holiday Inn in the world looked the same as every other, so it hardly mattered what city you were in," she agreed.

"Certainly when I travelled professionally there was little time or opportunity to explore. Always people to meet, functions to attend, and a specific role that I was forced to play. It was much more rewarding when I had the opportunity to travel on my own terms."

"I've always wanted to travel more," my mother said.

"Then what stops you?" he asked.

"I guess there's work, and of course the kids."

"I know of no country that does not welcome children as visitors. Your children are not anchors to hold you in place, *madame*, but wings to help you soar."

"You make it all sound so easy," she said, with a bit of a laugh.

He shrugged. "It can be."

"Well, maybe you're right, but right now the only place my little one should travel to is bed."

"Mom …," Jennie mumbled, "I'm not a baby!" She was sitting curled up beside our mother and had nearly fallen asleep. Her eyes were closed and she was drawing in long, soft breaths through her open mouth. Typical—even when she was falling asleep she couldn't keep her mouth closed.

"She's exhausted," my mother said.

"It was a long paddle," Pierre said. "She was a real *voyageur.*"

"A what?" I asked.

"The original fur traders travelled throughout this country in canoes. They were called *les voyageurs*."

"And they were French, right?" my mother said.

"Yes."

"And you speak French?" my mother asked.

"It is one of my languages. And your husband?"

"He always said he spoke *street* French."

Pierre laughed out loud. I'd seen him smile and smirk and even chuckle, but that was the first time I'd heard a real, honest-to-goodness belly laugh.

"He didn't get much chance to use it in New York," she added.

"Spanish would have been more helpful, I'm sure," Pierre said.

"He spoke some Spanish, too," I said.

"Just a bit," my mother said. "He always spoke to our cleaning woman in Spanish ... or at least tried. She loved him for that."

"Often the effort is as important as the result," Pierre said.

My mother got up, pulling Jennie to her feet as she did. "Bedtime, my little *voyageur*."

"Do I *have* to?" Jennie whined.

"Yes, and I think I should try to get to sleep as well. Come on." She led Jennie, half stumbling in the dark, toward the tent. "Good night."

"*Bonne nuit* … good night."

She stopped just before she got to the tent and turned around. "Brian, you won't stay up too long … right?"

"Is that a question or an order?"

"A little of both."

"Not too much longer."

"Good. You need your rest too."

She bent down and she and Jennie disappeared into the tent.

I was tired, but I knew there wasn't much point in going to bed. It seemed more right to *not* sleep sitting up than it did to *not* sleep lying down. So we continued to sit around the fire, not talking. Pierre always seemed comfortable with the silence. I wasn't. Even though I wasn't crazy about being alone, I'd have been happier if he'd just gone to bed and left me by myself. It seemed more right to *not* talk when *nobody* was there.

"Your father, how did he die?"

I don't know which surprised me more—the fact that he was starting a conversation or what he'd chosen to open with. The guy was really not good at small talk.

"I'm sorry … what?" He'd surprised me so much I didn't know what to answer.

"How did your father die? If you would rather not talk about it, I understand."

"No, it's okay, I guess. It was a car accident. He was on his way home from work—it was late—he hit a pole."

"Fast. Sudden. Unexpected. No time to say goodbye."

Everybody had told me that he wouldn't have suffered, that death would have been instant. I just remember him heading out the door that morning when I was getting up. I saw him for, like, twenty seconds. He said something about watching the Knicks on TV with me that night. And for the longest time I thought about what I would have said to him if I'd known I was never going to see him again. Then I realized: if I'd known that, I would have told him not to go to work.

"They say a sudden death is easier for the person who dies and harder for the people who are left behind."

I didn't know what to say to that, either. I just knew I didn't want to talk about any of it. I picked up a stick and poked the fire, sending embers flying to join the stars. I stared up into the sky—an uncountable array of stars. We sat for a while in uncomfortable silence.

"You ever wonder about what's up there?" I asked, pointing skyward.

"Do you?"

"I guess I wouldn't ask the question if I didn't."

"And what do you think is up there?" he asked.

"I don't think, I *know*. Scientists know. There are thousands and thousands of stars and planets, but mostly it's just empty space—deep, dark, cold space that goes on forever."

"*The eternal silence of these infinite spaces fills me with dread.*"

"What?"

"Pascal."

"Friend of yours?"

He chuckled, and I felt embarrassed. "French philosopher. Does that infinite space frighten you?"

I almost blurted out no, but I didn't. "Sometimes … if I think about it too much."

"Sometimes it frightens *me*," he said, "when I think about it too much."

We sat in silence again. The crackling of the fire was the only thing to disturb the quiet.

"It's hard to lose a parent," he said.

Obviously, at his age both of his parents were gone—long gone.

"My father died suddenly, like yours," he said. "I was fifteen. He went away and sent back word he was ill with pneumonia. And then he died. It was all so … so … unexpected." His voice wavered. "He was so alive, so formidable, and then he simply was … no more." He shook his head slowly.

I felt my whole chest tighten. That was so much like my father. How could somebody so strong just disappear from life?

"When I was told, in that split second I felt the whole world go empty," he said. "It was very traumatic. His death truly felt like the end of the world."

I felt my eyes start to water. I worked hard to stop the tears. I wasn't going to cry. I was tired of crying. I was through with it. Maybe I should just get up now, climb into my sleeping bag, and at least pretend to go to sleep.

"Do you believe that there is more than simply cold space above our heads?" he asked.

"What do you mean, like heaven?"

"Heaven, an afterlife. Do you believe?"

"I guess I do ... sometimes ... sort of," I said. "Do you?"

He didn't answer right away. He stared into the fire for the longest time, and I became more uncomfortable with each passing second.

Finally he said, "If you had asked me that a year ago, I would have answered with certainty. Now, I don't know. I hope. I'm just not so sure I believe anymore."

CHAPTER NINE

"THESE ARE SO GOOD," Jennie said as she popped another blueberry into her mouth.

"You're supposed to be picking, not eating," I said.

"I think she can do both," my mother said. She was picking berries a few bushes over.

"Besides, we're just picking them so we can eat them," Jennie said. "What did you think we were going to do, make jewellery with them?"

"We're supposed to save some, too," I told her. "This is not all about feeding your greedy face right now." I turned away so she couldn't see and popped a couple of berries in my mouth. They *were* good—ripe and juicy and sweet, and they practically melted in your mouth.

The berry patch was gigantic. I couldn't believe how big it was. It occupied the whole clearing. It was like a big bowl, surrounded by hills and hemmed in by the forest on all sides. You couldn't see it from the lake, and if Pierre hadn't known it was there, there was no way we would have found it. He'd told us that there had been a forest fire a few years ago, which had cleared the way for the blueberries and smaller bushes and saplings to grow. He said that forest fires could help regenerate a forest, that they were natural. All I knew about the subject was that Smokey the Bear always told us, "Only *you* can prevent forest fires." Living in New York City, that didn't really mean much to me. I believed Pierre over the talking cartoon bear, anyway.

Stopping to pick berries wasn't getting us any closer to where we needed to go, but we needed the berries to make up for the food we didn't have. We hadn't packed enough supplies to begin with, and then we'd lost half of them when my canoe had tipped going over the rapids.

Pierre was working his way through a stretch on the hill. He said that we didn't have to worry about food because the forest was filled with it. I hoped he wasn't being overly optimistic, because other than the berries, I hadn't yet seen anything I'd be willing to put in my mouth. I would have loved to have stumbled on a super-market, fast-food restaurant, or deli—actually, a New York deli would have been really fantastic, a nice corned beef sandwich with mustard ...

"What was that?" Jennie said.

I stopped picking and looked at her. She was wide-eyed and standing straight up.

"What was what?"

"I thought I saw something in the bushes," she said.

"Berries and maybe a bunny or—"

A black blur brushed by her leg and Jennie screamed! It was an animal—a bear—a tiny little bear cub! It disappeared into the bushes, but as it ran we could see the bushes twitching and moving as it rushed through them. We caught another quick glimpse of black fur as it reached the edge of the berry patch before disappearing into the forest.

"That was a bear!" Jennie gasped.

"Not a bear—a bear *cub*, and I think you scared it," I said.

"I scared *it*?"

"Maybe you scared each other."

"I was just startled, that's all," she said, defensively.

I knew that if it had shot by my leg I would have screamed as well, but I wasn't offering that piece of information.

"Actually, he was sort of cute," Jennie said. She started to laugh—not because she'd suddenly found it funny, I figured, but out of relief. I knew that bizarre emotion. At the funeral home, after we'd already been there for two nights—two late nights—while people came and paid their respects, somebody had said something to me, and it wasn't really funny, but I'd started laughing and couldn't stop.

"He looked just like Winnie the Pooh!"

"Let's just hope he didn't bring Tigger with him," I said. "I'm pretty sure I'm not ready to take on a tiger."

"Bears love berries," my mother said. She was laughing along with Jennie now.

"I'm just glad he was a cub ... but wait ... if there's a cub ... shouldn't there be a mother?" I asked anxiously.

Suddenly they both stopped laughing.

Slowly I turned, looking all around for the mother bear. She could have been anywhere—just behind those trees, or hidden by the thick bushes, or maybe just over the hill. But I couldn't see anything. There was nothing. Nothing at all. I let out a little sigh of relief—but just a little. Even if I couldn't see the bear right now, that didn't mean it wouldn't be here soon.

"Let's get out of here," I said.

Nobody argued. We started to walk, heading for the canoes. Getting berries to eat was one thing. The possibility of *being* eaten was another. But did we really have anything to be afraid of? I'd never heard of a bear eating anybody. They ate berries, so they had to be vegetarians, and so they wouldn't be interested in eating people ... right? But I ate berries ... *and* I ate meat. So much for trying to think it out.

"I'm sure there's nothing to worry about," my mother said, but she *sounded* worried. "We'll just keep moving and—"

We all saw the bear at the same instant, and we froze. It was large, black, and slowly lumbering forward, its nose to the ground. I suddenly had the strangest thought: it looked like one of those big, life-sized stuffed animals they always had on the first floor at FAO Schwartz on Fifth Avenue. They even had a big bear, along with a life-sized giraffe and lion and elephant. Tourists were always taking pictures of them, and the staff had to chase away the kids who tried to climb on top of them. Well, nobody was going to climb on top of this bear.

It kept coming forward, nose glued to the ground. Was it tracking its baby? It was headed to where we had been picking berries, directly to where the cub had appeared before it ran off. It didn't seem to have even noticed us yet. Maybe we could just ease away and it wouldn't even realize we were there.

Then it stopped and looked up, straight at us. I heard Jennie gasp.

In my head I tried to do some quick mathematical equations: How far away was the bear? How fast could it run? How fast could *we* run—could my mother run—and how far did we have to run to get to safety? It wasn't like we could run into a house or a building, and climbing a tree wouldn't help, because even I knew that bears could climb trees. What if we could get to the canoes? We could paddle away ... no, bears *had* to be able to swim. There was no safe place to run to. All we could do was stand there and hope it decided not to come any closer.

Out of nowhere, Pierre was at my side. He stepped forward so that he was standing between us and the bear.

"Don't move," he said calmly.

It was an easy order to follow. I didn't think I *could* move.

"Stand still."

He was talking to the wrong people. We were definitely standing still. It was the bear that was still moving—slowly, steadily, like a cat stalking a mouse ... and we were the mice.

Pierre stopped walking. He had put himself directly between us and the bear. That was brave, incredibly brave, but how was one old man with no weapon going to stop a bear? Maybe he could scare it or—

The bear charged!

I stood there, too scared to run, too stunned to think, and watched as this massive mound of black fury, growling and snarling, ran toward us, getting bigger and bigger and bigger! And just when I thought that we were all doomed, that I was going to find out about heaven and the afterlife sooner than I'd thought, it skidded to a stop, no more than two dozen feet in front of Pierre.

He just stood there, holding his ground, while the bear started to huff and snort. It pawed at the ground, ripping up dirt. Then, slowly, Pierre raised his hands above his head. It looked as though he was surrendering, giving up.

The bear just huffed loudly and charged again! This time when it skidded to a stop it was only a few feet in front of Pierre. He just stood there, not moving. The bear just stood there, not moving. They were practically eyeball to eyeball.

"I want you all to move … slowly … to the right," Pierre said. "Nobody run, and nobody turn away from the bear. Just back away … slowly."

I was terrified, but his voice was so calm, so reassuring, as if he were standing in line waiting for a coffee instead of facing down a wild bear. He was so calm that it calmed me down, too.

Slowly I slipped away to the side. Jennie didn't move. I reached out and grabbed her hand and gave her a tug. She whimpered but let me lead her. Our mother moved right with us.

The bear was staring directly at Pierre and he was staring at it. Neither of them noticed us. We kept moving, opening up space between us and them. Strangely, as the gap between us opened I was becoming *more* afraid. I should have felt better, but I didn't. I had to fight the urge to run … to leave my mother and sister behind, to run away from Pierre, leaving him alone to fight the bear. What a coward! I knew I should go back and—

Suddenly the bear charged at Pierre! He simply stepped to one side. The bear brushed past him and waddled up the hill until its big black backside disappeared into the forest, in the same place where the cub had disappeared.

I felt a rush of relief so strong that it almost melted my legs. I had to fight to stop from simply collapsing to the ground. Instead I started to stumble back toward Pierre. He motioned for me to stop and he rushed toward us instead.

"Are we safe … is it gone?" my mother asked.

"Safe, yes, but gone?" He shook his head. "Not far. Come. We have to get to the canoes." He started to walk.

"But that's not where the canoes are!" I said.

"You're right. The canoes are over there." He pointed in the opposite direction. "Where the bear and her cub have gone."

He was right. The cub had, by chance, gone up the hill straight toward our canoes. Without meaning to, when we'd tried to leave we'd put ourselves right between the mother bear and her cub. We'd been standing right where the bear wanted to go.

"This way is longer, but safer."

I wasn't going to argue. I fell in behind him, and my sister and mother followed me. I thought for a second that maybe I should be at the end of the line, to sort of defend us if the bear came back—like that was going to help anybody. Best to keep moving, I decided. I stumbled a couple of times. It was hard to move forward while looking nervously over my shoulder.

We all crowded in close to Pierre. That wasn't just because of the bear. Losing sight of him might mean getting lost. The ground was rough and uneven and he had to continually change his path to find a way around. We would have been lost almost immediately, but I just knew he knew where he was going. We certainly weren't moving in anything close to a straight line—in fact, it seemed as though we were tracing a gigantic, looping circle. That made sense. That would get us back to the lake some place wide of where the canoes were beached. Then we could work our way along the shore and avoid the bear ... probably ... most likely ... I hoped.

There was a loud snap and I practically jumped, spinning around.

"That was just me," Jennie said. "Sorry."

"It's okay."

"I guess we're all a little nervous," she said.

Nervous was certainly a step down from terrified, which was how we'd all been feeling ... all of us except Pierre. He had been like some kind of comic book hero. No, I knew exactly who he reminded me of.

"The way you stood up to that bear, Pierre, you were like Davy Crockett."

"Ah, yes, the famous American frontiersman."

"He even wore a buckskin jacket like yours. I read that he killed his first bear when he was only three years old."

"That sounds improbable."

"It's part of the legend," I said. "He was brave, he wasn't afraid of anything, like you weren't afraid of that bear."

"You think I was not afraid?" he asked.

"You *were* afraid?"

"To not be afraid would have been a total lapse of reason and judgment. That was a large, angry mother bear."

"But you didn't move, you didn't back up. You didn't *act* scared."

"*Being* scared and *acting* scared are two different things. You can win some confrontations just by acting confident. One thing I learned as a boy is that it is important to stand up to any bully. If the bear had sensed my fear, it would have attacked."

"And it could have killed you," I said.

"That was a possibility."

"But you still stood there."

"One must be prepared to fight the good fight, regardless of the odds of winning, or even the certainty of the loss. At the least it would have bought time for you three to flee."

"When you were standing in front of the bear, why did you raise your hands above your head?" I asked.

"I wanted the bear to think I was bigger than I really am. I needed to be perceived as being larger. Most animals see height as strength. You must know the thoughts of your opponent, whether it is a bear or a man."

"I think that was the bravest thing I ever saw," Jennie said.

"Are you referring to me or to the bear?" Pierre asked.

"You, of course!" she exclaimed.

"Do not underestimate the bravery of the bear. She stood toe to toe with me, willing to risk her life."

"But it was a bear, a big bear with big teeth and razor-sharp claws. She could have ripped your head off."

"She had equal cause to fear us. She had every reason to believe that I would kill her, yet she was willing to fight, one against four, against these strange, unknown creatures, with weapons or powers of which she had no knowledge." He stopped walking and paused, as though he was thinking. "But then, what mother would not put her life at risk for her children? Would you not agree?" he asked my mother.

"In a heartbeat," she said.

"Until you have children, you may not realize the power," he said.

"Do you have children?" my mother asked.

"Yes. Four…" He looked as though he was going to say something else, but he didn't.

I hated silence. "Boys or girls?" I asked, filling the gap.

"Three boys and a girl."

"They must be all grown up," my mother said.

"The boys, yes, but my daughter is the age of your daughter."

"But … but Jennie's only nine."

"As is my daughter, Sarah."

"You have a nine-year-old?" I said without thinking.

"Yes. You sound surprised."

I *was* surprised. And judging from the expression on my mother's face, I wasn't the only one.

"You must wonder how it is that a man of my age— an old man—could possibly have such a young child. Is that what you are thinking?"

"No, of course not!" I exclaimed, trying to be polite.

"That's what *I* would be thinking," he said.

"Well," my mother said, "it is … a little unusual."

"One does not question the blessings that God bestows, one merely accepts them. My children are the greatest blessings of my life. Sarah is just another blessing, later in my life."

"I'm sure she is," my mother agreed.

"I'm sure she would love to be here now. All of my children have a love of the outdoors."

"That must bring you great joy," my mother said.

"Yes. Great joy. And great regret."

Regret? What was that supposed to mean? What was he trying to say? That was something I'd noticed. He often left things unsaid, or half said, and most of the time when he was asked a question he answered with a question of his own.

Pierre came to a stop and I stood beside him, and then felt my knees turn to jelly. We were standing on top of a cliff, the lake far below us. I stepped back a half-step.

"You do not like heights?" he asked.

"Not when I don't know they're coming." We had to be twenty-five feet above the water.

"It's a beautiful sight," my mother said.

The whole lake was visible, framed by forest and rocks, blue water and blue sky. It looked like a picture postcard.

"There's a path here that cuts down to the lake," Pierre said.

"Doesn't it look as if we could just jump into the water?" Jennie said.

"Not possible. The water is only a few feet deep, here. You can tell by the colour."

"If we could have jumped that would have been fun," I said. Now that I knew we couldn't, I figured it was safe to say it.

"You would enjoy jumping into the lake from a height like this?" Pierre asked.

"That would be incredible!" Jennie said.

"Yeah ... it would be ... great," I said, trying to conceal my concern.

Pierre didn't say anything, but there was a slight smile on his face. Funny, that smile did not bring a smile to *my* face.

We moved along the top of the cliff. I tried to focus on my feet. The path was rough and uneven, with loose rocks along the way. It wasn't reassuring to know that if we did fall there wasn't enough water to catch us. The path descended quickly and soon we were at the water's edge. Pierre wound his way along the shoreline. At times the way was blocked and we had to move inland, out of sight of the water. It was never far or for long, but each time it happened I felt my anxiety rise. In sight of the water somehow seemed safer, as if the water was our getaway route. Maybe bears could swim, but they couldn't hide in the water the way they could hide in the woods.

"I think we should all sing," Pierre suggested.

"You want us to sing?" Now I'd heard everything!

"Yes. We need to make more noise, in case the bear is close."

"Shouldn't we try to be *quiet* in case it's close?"

He laughed. "If she hears us, she will have time to run."

"And by run, you mean run away, right?"

He laughed again. "That would be the hope."

He began to sing. There was no chance any of us were going to join in. It wasn't just that we didn't know the song, we didn't even know the language. He was singing in French. It did seem like a bouncy, happy sort of song. He sang louder and louder until we broke through the last little line of trees and found ourselves on the patch of sand. And there, right there, were our canoes.

CHAPTER TEN

"YOU ARE FEELING much better today," Pierre said.

"Yes, I am." My ribs were still a little tender, but not enough to stop me from paddling. We'd been out on the water since first light, and I'd been trying to do my share all day. If we really had to do this trip, at least I could make myself useful.

"Your stroke would be more effective if you used a different technique. Who taught you to paddle?"

"My counsellors at camp, I guess. But really, this isn't brain surgery," I said. "It's just pushing a piece of wood through the water to make the canoe go forward. Basic physics. Push the water back and the canoe goes forward."

"It is good to know that you are a student of physics," he said. "But physics also tells us that you would have more power if you slipped your lower hand farther down the shank of the paddle."

I looked at my hands. The last thing in the world I wanted was a lesson or a lecture.

"Go ahead, try. You will see that I am right."

Reluctantly I let one hand slip down the shaft of the paddle. I dipped it in the water for a stroke. It did feel as though I had more power, or, really, as though the force was being shared more evenly between the two arms.

"Doesn't that feel better?"

"Sure, I guess so."

"Now you just have to work on the stroke itself. Try to keep your paddle closer to the side of the canoe. It's harder on the muscles if you have to extend a greater distance."

"Anything else?" I asked, feeling a bit annoyed.

"You could dip more of the paddle's blade into the water. Your stroke is not deep enough."

"Is there anything that I'm doing that you *do* think is right?"

"Well, you are holding it by the correct end."

"Thanks. Maybe you should be giving this lesson to my mother and sister."

"Perhaps."

"Maybe my sister should be here with you and I could paddle with my mother. Now that my side isn't hurting so much, we could move faster that way."

"Tomorrow we might change partners. For now, this is good. But speaking of partners reminds me that I wanted to ask you about something," Pierre said. "You have dual citizenship, but you feel that you are an American, not a Canadian. Is that correct?"

"I don't *feel*. I *am*. I was born and raised in the U.S. of A."

"But you have no sense of your Canadian heritage?"

"My father might have been Canadian, but I've hardly ever even been up here."

"Then this trip might change your perception. I know many men who had no sense of patriotism but acquired that virtue when they felt in their bones the vastness of this land, and the greatness of those who founded it."

"That would make a great bumper sticker ... if your bumper was really big. Canada's bigger than America, right? I mean, just in terms of land mass."

"Much larger."

"But not more powerful," I said.

"No country ever has been. The United States is arguably the most powerful country the world has ever seen, and we Canadians are, in some ways, fortunate to have it as a neighbour."

"Some ways?" I asked. "Does that mean in other ways you're not so fortunate?"

"We are the mouse that lives in the shadow of the giant. If the giant rolls over, it is the mouse that will be crushed. What confuses me is why you can't see yourself as belonging to *both* countries."

"I don't think you can belong to both," I said. "Either you're one thing or another."

"You're wrong."

Two words, delivered with complete confidence. It was certainly what I had come to expect from Pierre. Sometimes that confidence was what was needed— knowing the right route, finding food for us to eat, facing a bear. But sometimes it was more like a weapon aimed at you, and you got both barrels of it square between the eyes.

"How would you know?" I snapped. "You were born and raised here, right?"

"My whole life."

"Then you wouldn't understand what it's like to be caught in the middle."

He chuckled. "Do you know about the history of this country?" he asked.

"Not really."

"I'm not surprised. Americans often know little about the world beyond their borders. Let me explain. You are familiar with the fact that Canada has two founding peoples."

"I'm not even sure what that means," I said.

"Two peoples, speaking two languages, settled this country."

"French and English, right?"

"Yes, the two languages spoken by your father."

"He mainly spoke English, though."

"Most people are better at one language than the other, although it is possible to be fluently bilingual."

"You speak both languages, so which one are you better at?"

"I feel that I am equally fluent in both. My mother was English and my father French. I have always, as far back as I can recall, been able to speak both languages. They merged seamlessly in my home and in my life."

"But you must speak one better than the other, feel more comfortable with one," I said.

He shook his head. "You are wrong."

Again, that irritating certainty, like he was 100 percent certain that he was right and I was wrong. I figured he probably ticked a lot of people off with that attitude.

"In Quebec, many people speak both languages, but the majority of the people have French as their mother tongue. In the rest of the country, English is almost always the dominant language."

"But my father spoke English, and he was from Quebec."

"He was in the minority. It has long been the belief of many French-speaking people in Quebec that our province—because of its language, its history, its culture —is distinct, different from the rest of Canada. So different, in fact, that it should be a separate country."

"You mean like ... leave Canada?"

"Yes, their dream is for Quebec to separate from the rest of Canada and stand alone as an independent nation."

"And that would be allowed? They could do that?"

"Most advocated peaceful measures to pursue their goals. A small minority chose to pursue violence."

"Violence?"

"Yes, there were bombings, people were kidnapped, a politician was murdered."

I couldn't believe that. I'd never heard anything about it. When I thought about Canada I imagined a peaceful place with friendly Mounties and maple syrup ... but then again, there was sure nothing gentle about hockey.

"It was necessary for the federal government to step in, bring in troops, suspend the rights of its citizens."

"I just can't believe that could happen here."

"It was hard for all of us to believe. It was a long time ago ... almost thirty years ... but still there is anger, bitterness. Those who chose violence were a small, angry group. The real danger of separation was not through bullets but through ballots."

"You mean like an election?"

"It was called a referendum. People were given the choice of staying or leaving."

"But didn't most of the people in the country want Quebec to stay?" I asked.

"Almost all of the people in Canada, but only the people of Quebec, the *Québécois*, were given a vote."

"That doesn't seem fair. It's about the whole country."

"Even more unfair, those seeking to leave did not have the courage to ask the simple question, 'Do you wish to stay or leave?' The question that the people of Quebec voted on was written in language that made it seem possible to leave Canada but retain all the rights and privileges of being Canadian."

"That doesn't make sense."

"You might well argue that the separatists were appealing not to reason but to emotion."

"But in the end, Quebec chose to stay, right?"

"Both times."

"This happened more than once?"

"Twice. In 1980, and then again in 1995."

"But that was just four years ago!"

"It seems like only yesterday. And it almost worked. The forces of separation were defeated by less than 1 percent."

"Wow, that was close. So if they had won, then Quebec would be another country now."

"I like to believe not. The rest of Canada would ultimately have had a say, and the people of Quebec would have learned what separation would truly mean. Then there is the whole question of the Native peoples. Even if Quebec had been successful in leaving, you might *still* be in a part of Canada right now, because the northern peoples, the Native Canadians, voted overwhelmingly to remain in Canada."

"I can't believe people were allowed to just vote like that on something so important," I said.

"And yet the United States was born when its people rose up against a powerful country and declared their independence as a nation. Should people today not have the same right to choose how they will be governed and what is important to them as a nation?"

"Well, yeah, but it's not like every farmer in the Thirteen Colonies was asked on a ballot whether he wanted to be British or American. These days there's no excuse for not giving everyone all the important information and making decisions fairly and openly and letting everyone have a say."

"Democracy. It is the worst form of government ... except for all others that have been tried. Winston Churchill said that."

"Him I know. He was the British prime minister in the olden days."

"Yes. He was a great politician, though many people do not believe the words *great* and *politician* can go together."

"You worked for the government. Did you have a lot to do with politicians?"

"Far more than I would have liked. Some were true leaders, and others were simply self-serving. The issue of separatism divided the country; it divided the province. It created bitterness between people, even those who had been neighbours, friends, and relatives. Many people argued that you could not be both *Québécois* and Canadian. That you had to be one or the other. And this was a painful idea."

"But you said your mother was English and your father was French ... I guess *Québécois*, like you said."

He smiled. Suddenly I understood what he meant.

"I am French—*Québécois*—and I am Canadian. I am both," he said.

"So you didn't want Quebec to separate, right?"

"You could say that I played a part in fighting against that separation. Canada is a country of limitless promise. A land perhaps on the threshold of greatness. To divide the country would be to divide that promise, to limit that greatness."

"I'm just glad it didn't work."

"Why?"

"Canada is my father's country. He was proud of it."

"As *you* should be proud. There is no need to turn your back on your heritage. To do so is to turn your back on a part of who your father was ... and who you might become. Never let anybody, including yourself, define your limits, deny the totality of what you may become."

We paddled along in silence. I understood what he meant. I just wasn't sure yet if he was right.

CHAPTER ELEVEN

WE SAT IN THE CANOE, gently bobbing up and down in the shade of a tall cliff of red rocks, waiting for my mother and Jennie to catch us. That was the pattern. We'd take the lead and then wait for them to catch up. We never left them too far behind.

There was no conversation now. Pierre hadn't said much for the last two or three hours. I hadn't said anything much either. Partly I was just playing a game, proving he wasn't the only one who could keep quiet. That wasn't all of it, though. I was comfortable being alone with my thoughts, and Pierre was pretty good at putting something into my head to think about.

Jennie and my mother came up slowly. I watched the way they paddled—slow and choppy and awkward. They could have used a lesson or two from Pierre. Heck, *I* could have shown them how to do it better now. They came up beside us, bumping us gently, and I grabbed on to the side of their canoe.

"How are you two doing?" Pierre asked.

"Okay," my mother said.

"I'm tired," Jennie said.

"It has been a long day. We'll stop for the night just up ahead."

"But isn't the camp close to here?" I asked.

"Perhaps three hours away."

We might have been able to go a little farther—judging from the position of the sun in the sky we probably had a couple of hours of light left—but I was sure he was right. He usually was.

Pierre angled our canoe toward a flat spot on the shore. What I'd learned from sharing a canoe with him was that, sitting in the stern, he had complete control over the direction we travelled. I could add some power and speed, but he was in control. I think he liked to be in control ... no, I didn't just think so, I *knew* so.

We came up to the shore and I hopped out of the canoe and into the knee-deep water. It was cold, but the cold felt good. Pierre climbed out as well. For a split second he seemed to lose his balance, and I thought he was going to fall, but he managed to steady himself against the canoe. I dragged it up onto the shore while Pierre waited for the others. As soon as he could reach their canoe he took the bow and guided it in, bringing it right up onto the sandy shore. He offered a hand first to my sister and then to my mother, so that neither even needed to get her feet wet.

I started to undo the ties that were securing our supplies in the canoe.

"I was thinking that we could set up camp quickly so we might have time for a swim," Pierre suggested.

"I'd like to go for a swim," I said.

"Me too!" Jennie squealed.

"I think I'll pass," my mother said. "I just want to sit still for a little while and forget what it feels like to have a paddle in my hand."

"Perhaps you'll want to come and watch, though," he said.

"She's seen us swim before," I told him.

"I'm sure she has. But she might be very interested in seeing how you are going to enter the water."

"I don't understand."

"Well, you could just slip into the water," he said, "but perhaps you might want to jump in." He pointed at the cliffs. "From there."

"Yeah, right," I chuckled.

He shook his head. "No, I'm serious. The water is deep right off the drop. It's quite safe."

"I'm not sure this is a wise idea," my mother said.

I had to agree with her, but I didn't say anything. I didn't want to look like a suck.

"I understand your concern, but people jump from these rocks all the time."

"People? What people?" I asked.

"Well, many years ago, probably your father. This is one of the activities they used to have the campers do every year. Just come, look."

CAREFULLY I CLIMBED UP the face of the cliff. It rose straight out of the water, and while it was steep, there were hand- and footholds. Pierre reached down and offered me a hand. His grip was strong, and he hauled me up onto a ledge beside Jennie. It wasn't wide—no more than two feet—but it was certainly wide enough to be a safe place to stand.

I bent over slightly and looked over the edge. We were fifteen or twenty feet above the water. It was dark and blue and I couldn't see the bottom. I guessed that was good. That meant it was deep ... didn't it? Before we'd climbed, Pierre had taken a swim at the base of the cliff. Several times he'd dived beneath the surface—sometimes he was underwater for ten or fifteen seconds—checking to make sure there were no logs floating just under the surface, or any other hazards. He'd said it was clear.

"What does it look like from up there?" my mother called. She was standing down below, off to the side.

"It's a nice view!" I called back.

"Does it look safe?"

"Sure ... I guess."

"It *is* safe," Pierre insisted. "The water is more than twenty feet deep straight off the rocks."

"Can I go first?" Jennie asked.

After that, there was no possibility of me even suggesting that we shouldn't go without looking like a complete and utter wimp.

"Sure, why not," I said.

Pierre got down on one knee right beside Jennie. "There's nothing to be afraid of."

"I'm not afraid."

"Good girl. When you jump, I want you to try to enter the water with your legs together and your hands above your head. Show me."

She stood up straight, with her arms up.

"Jumping like that will make the entry smooth, but you will go deep. Just hold your breath and you will rise to the surface."

"I know."

"You don't have to do this if it makes you uncomfortable," Pierre said.

"I *want* to do this."

"Right, then." Jennie looked ready to go, but she still stood there.

"Brian?" she said.

I recognized her scared voice, even if Pierre didn't. I didn't really want to get any closer to the edge, but maybe I could help her. I had to admit it, she was a pretty tough kid, and kind of brave, and the least I could do as her big brother was help her feel safe.

"It's okay, Jen." I took her hand and guided her to the edge. "It's really not dangerous. You just put your arms straight up, like Pierre said, and take a deep breath. You can do it."

She lifted her hands above her head. For a split second I had the terrible thought that she was going to *dive* instead of jump. And then she just did it—she just jumped! I leaned over in time to see her enter the water, and a plume of water shot up as she disappeared under the surface. A few seconds passed and then she popped back up to the top.

"That was fun!" she screamed.

"Bravo!" Pierre called out. "Bravo!"

I clapped my hands and screamed out approval!

Jennie treaded water for a bit and then swam over to the shore. I was impressed! My mother was waiting there with a towel and gave her a big hug.

"I guess I'm next," I said.

"I was wondering, how old was your father when he attended the camp?"

"I think he was ten the first time, and he came for four or five years. Why?"

"Your sister jumped from the lower ledge. That's the place where first- or second-year campers would have jumped, the place your father would have jumped when he was ten or eleven. In your father's last two or three years, when he was your age, he would have jumped from up there."

I looked up to where he was pointing. The cliff went up another ten or fifteen feet.

"Come."

He started to climb again. He hadn't asked me if I wanted to go any higher. He'd just assumed I did. I didn't.

The climb up to the next level was as easy as the first. I could picture hundreds of campers in swimsuits making this same climb over the years. I thought about my father doing it. Funny, I couldn't imagine him at my age, even though I'd seen pictures. Instead, in my mind he looked just the way he had that morning ... that last morning.

I climbed up to the top of the cliff. Pierre was standing there, bent over, his hands on his waist.

"Quite the climb," he said.

He looked as though he was kind of short of breath... and was he shaking? It was easy to forget most of the time that he was really kind of an old guy.

"Take care at the edge," Pierre warned.

I didn't need the warning. I stood back a few feet. There was lots of space behind us, and the ground sloped gently away, disappearing into bushes and trees.

"From the lower level, you simply step out into space and wait until you hit the water," Pierre said. "From this level, though, it is necessary to jump out to ensure that you clear the outreach of the lower ledge."

Carefully I looked over the edge. I could see what he meant.

"Do you like heights?" Pierre asked.

I shook my head. "Not particularly. But this isn't *really* high." At least I could *sound* brave.

"About the height of a balcony. I could picture Roxanne standing at this height."

"Roxanne?"

"A character in the story of Cyrano de Bergerac."

"I don't know the story."

"Cyrano was a real man, a Parisian born in the sixteenth century. He was blessed with the skills of a swordsman and the power of poetry, but cursed with an abundantly bulbous nose—a nose so large that he could never win the affections of his love, the beautiful Roxanne."

"She wouldn't love him because he had a big nose?"

"An *enormous* nose."

"It still seems pretty lame ... pretty shallow."

"Roxanne was far too concerned with appearances. She was infatuated with another man, a friend of Cyrano's, Christian de Neuvillette. He was most handsome in his appearance, but dull and slow in his speech. Cyrano offered to assist his friend in securing the heart of Roxanne."

"He helped his friend get the girl that *he* was in love with?"

"Exactly."

"Well, that's stupid."

"Some might say it was noble," Pierre said.

"Nope," I said. "Just plain stupid."

"While the lovely Roxanne was perched on her balcony, Christian was below, offering his words of love. What Roxanne did not know, however, was that these words were being given to him by Cyrano, who was hiding in the shadows."

"Sounds like this Cyrano was quite a sap," I said.

"Far from it!" Pierre said. He sounded genuinely upset. "Cyrano was a man of action, of romance. A man so skilled with his sword that he could fight against overwhelming odds and still triumph!"

"Okay, so he was good at fighting, but in the end did he get Roxanne?" I asked.

"Well …," he said, and shrugged. "Maybe he was afraid. He was willing to help someone else take a risk, but he was afraid to face his own true feelings, his own fears, the fear that she would not care for him."

"Then he was a sap." I wasn't quite sure why he'd told me all that. Maybe just to take my mind off the height? It didn't really help. "Have *you* ever jumped from here?" I asked.

"*Jumped*? No, I have never jumped, but I have seen it done. We could climb back down to the level where your sister jumped, if you like."

"No, I want to do it."

"Do you want me to go first?" he asked.

I shook my head. If he went first, I didn't know if I'd be able to go at all, and I really did want to go. I couldn't let my little sister show me up. Besides, knowing my father, I knew *he* would have done it. He would have jumped off the highest ledge. That was just him. He would have done it, and he would have *loved* it.

I slowly crept out to the edge. It was high. The rocks sloped down sharply, with the lower ledge being the only thing extending out from the surface of the cliff. Below that, the water was dark, smooth. There wasn't a ripple. It looked like glass.

I'd seen my sister jump. I knew the water was deep enough. Well, deep enough for a jump from half this height. But Pierre had told me it was deep enough and he knew ... although he'd never jumped from here ... but he had seen people jump. My mind kept bouncing back and forth, thinking of reasons why it was okay and why it wasn't.

"You can still change your mind—"

"No."

I looked across the lake. The sun was going down quickly and its rays were shimmering, reflecting off the water. It was starting to disappear behind the trees on the far side of the lake. It was ... beautiful. Beautiful in a way that no city was ever beautiful. I could imagine that I was all alone—no one else in sight. It was just me, and the cliff, and the water ... and a challenge. I tried to see the scene through my father's eyes, imagine what he might have felt, standing right here. He'd have jumped—I knew he would have. So why couldn't I?

Pierre looked hard into my face with his piercing blue eyes. "You're afraid—is that it?" he said.

That was enough. I didn't want to listen to him anymore.

I stepped forward, raised my hands above my head, and jumped! I felt myself falling, my heart rising up into my throat, and then I sliced into the water! I went down, down, down, and then stopped. I kicked my legs and pulled with my arms until I rose up and broke the surface!

My mother and Jennie were clapping and hooting, and I heard Pierre yelling out his congratulations. I took a deep breath and then put my head down and swam over to the shore. I started thinking that this was the first time I'd been in the water since the rapids. Probably best I hadn't thought about that. I waded out and grabbed a towel, and my mother and sister both gave me a big hug.

"Did you like it?" Jennie asked.

"Yeah, it was good." I was actually surprised that I could honestly say that.

"Do you think I could do it again?" she asked our mother.

"Not tonight. It'll be dark soon."

Good answer. If Jennie went again, maybe I'd be expected to do the same. It was exciting, but once was enough, for now. I looked up at the top of the cliff. The sun was going down so fast that Pierre was just a silhouette against the sky.

"He'd better jump soon or it'll be dark," Jennie said.

He lifted his arms above his head. He was getting ready. He stood perfectly still. Was he thinking better of it? Wouldn't that be something, if I'd made the jump but he was afraid? Then he launched himself off the cliff— but he wasn't jumping, he was diving! Head first he plummeted toward the lake! He sliced into the water with barely a splash. Then he surfaced, and we all gave a collective sigh. He started swimming toward us. We all stood there, too stunned to talk.

"The water is wonderful," he said with a huge smile as he waded out.

"I can't believe you dived!" I said.

"As I said, I have never jumped from there before ... but I have dived many times."

CHAPTER TWELVE

THE CAMPFIRE CRACKLED NOISILY. I was enjoying the silence of the night, the cool of the air. I felt sunburned, achy, and completely exhausted but, strangely, for the first time on this trip, I felt ... right. I'd made the jump, and I'd kind of surprised myself, too. I'd never seen myself as the woodsy, outdoorsy, jumping-off-cliffs kind of guy. I guess I was actually beginning to enjoy the wilderness life. I'd even stopped thinking about home and wondering how the Mets were doing—well, maybe not entirely.

Jennie was snuggled in against my mother.

"Is she asleep?" I asked softly.

"I'm awake," she murmured. "I just had my eyes closed. I was thinking about the bear."

"The bear is far away," Pierre said.

"I know. I was just thinking about the cub. It was cute."

"*You're* cute," my mother said.

"I know."

We all chuckled.

"And I bet that baby bear is tucked into bed right now," my mother said. "And maybe my baby bear should go to bed too. Okay?"

"Okay," she said, sleepily.

My mother got up and started to lead Jennie away.

"Wait." Jennie walked back over to Pierre. She wrapped her arms around him and gave him a kiss on the cheek. "Good night."

"Good night, little one."

She and my mother went into the tent and zipped up the flap behind them. Leaving me with Pierre ... with nothing to do but talk. He made me a bit nervous, because I never knew what he was going to say next. Maybe it was time for me to—

"She is a sweet little girl. The death of your father must have been very difficult for her. For all of you," he began.

I didn't know what to say. What I did know was that I was sure I didn't want to talk about any of *this*. I got up, grabbed another log, and tossed it into the fire, sending a cloud of smoke and ash into the air.

"The death of my father was one of the hardest blows of my life," he went on. "To this day, I cannot go to a funeral without crying."

"I'm never going to another funeral," I snapped.

"We never wish to attend funerals, but often we have no choice. Wishes do not change reality."

I felt my chest tightening up. I'd had too much reality lately and not enough wishes-come-true.

"I'm going to go to bed," I said. I stood up and turned my back to him, hoping he'd take the hint. But he didn't.

"You can go to bed," he said, "but you won't be able to sleep. Pulling the covers over your eyes does not stop your mind from thinking."

"What?" I asked, spinning back to face him.

"You cannot escape your thoughts. You must face the truth, the pain of your father's death."

I felt my whole body tingle and my spine stiffen. "You think you understand what I'm going through?" I snapped.

"I think I do."

"Do you really think you have a clue what I'm feeling today just because your father died a hundred years ago?" I demanded.

"It does feel like a hundred years ago … and only yesterday. But that's not why I understand how you are trying to escape."

"Then why do you think you know?"

"Because since my son died, I have wanted to escape, too."

"Your son?"

"My youngest boy. He died last year. And it was as if the world had ended."

"I ... I didn't know," I sputtered.

He shrugged. "How could you?"

He got up and turned away for a moment, gathering a few more branches for the campfire. "It's been almost ten months," I heard him say. "So unexpected ... so sudden."

"How did it happen?" I asked, surprising myself by the question.

He came back and sat down by the fire again. "He was out skiing with his friends in the mountains, doing what he loved. It was an accident. An avalanche. He was swept to his death."

"I'm so sorry."

"Thank you."

I came back and sat down opposite him, the fire separating us. He was staring, eyes wide open, into the fire. He looked lost, confused. He also looked tired and old and sad ... no, *sad* wasn't the right word. He looked defeated.

"When we first met, when I first spoke to you and your mother, I was very angry," Pierre said. "I could not believe that you would risk your lives so foolishly, so thoughtlessly."

"We just didn't know."

"I know, but that didn't stop the anger I felt. My son ... he was very knowledgeable about the wilderness, and *still* it took him."

I knew he was right. I'd tried to put it out of my mind, but I did know how close I had come to drowning.

"He loved the outdoors. We spent so much time together. My career was demanding but I tried to be a good father and—"

"You *were* a good father," I said, cutting him off. "I'm sure you must have been. And your son must have thought so, too."

Pierre looked up at me. He didn't speak, but there was a faint smile on the edges of his lips. He nodded ever so slightly.

"When you said you taught your children to love the outdoors," I said, "is that what you meant about *regret?*"

"I suppose it is. I've always believed regret to be a useless emotion, but it is so much a part of human nature."

I flashed back to my father the morning he died, how he'd left for work, how I wished I could have told him not to go.

"I think I understand," I said. "And I think I'm beginning to understand why your son loved the outdoors so much. Why my father loved it up here so much."

He smiled. "This is heaven."

"I thought you weren't sure if there was a heaven," I said.

He didn't speak right away. I could see in the light from the fire that his eyes were closed, his expression thoughtful.

"There was a time when I was as certain of heaven and hell as I am of my own existence. I was a true believer."

"And you stopped believing because of what happened to your son?"

"I don't know if I stopped as much as I began to question. Are you familiar with the Bible?"

That question caught me completely by surprise. "We go to church sometimes. I know about Adam and Eve and Moses ... and, you know, Jesus."

"Do you know the story of Job?"

I shook my head.

"It is a long and complicated story, but I'll try to explain. Job was a very devout man who believed in God and tried to obey his will. He was also wealthy and blessed with ten children. God was proud of Job's devotion, but Satan said that Job was devoted to God only because God had given him so much. God wanted to prove that Satan was wrong, so he allowed Satan to strip away all of Job's possessions and take all of his children—kill them. But in spite of losing everything, Job still believed in God and remained devout. Since Job remained true, God returned all his possessions and blessed him with ten more children."

"Okay, I know that story. That's why they say some-body is being tested like Job when lots of bad things happen, right?" I asked.

"Exactly. This is the book of the Bible that has been most on my mind over the past months." He paused again. "When you are as old as I—"

"You're not that old."

He smiled. A sad smile. "I will soon be eighty years of age. I am old. There comes a time when you are ready to die," he said, the words coming slowly and softly. "I was prepared for death." He paused and took a deep breath. "What I was not prepared for was the death of my son."

"I'm just so sorry," I said. I didn't know what else to say. Anyway, that's what people had said to me—the ones that said anything at all. With some people it was like they were afraid, like if they said anything about my father I'd break down, or maybe they would.

"Brian, you didn't want to be here because it meant you'd have to think about why you came, about what happened to your father, and face your own feelings. I came up here because I wanted to think, to feel," Pierre said. "I wanted to be alone with nature and, by doing that, be with my son."

"And then we came along and ruined it."

He shook his head vigorously. "Not ruined. Changed. Changed for the better. You have helped me by letting me help you. I should thank you and your mother and sister."

"Thank us? We should thank you!"

"You have."

"I don't know what we would have done without you, or how we can repay you."

"You *have* repaid me." He stood up, walked around the fire, and put a hand on my shoulder. "Now it is time for me to sleep. Good night."

CHAPTER THIRTEEN

I COULD JUST SEE my mother and Jennie in the distance. From where I stood on the shore they were a small dot, getting smaller and smaller as they paddled across the lake and away from us. They had started early, while Pierre and I stayed behind to finish breaking down the camp. Since we paddled so much faster, if we left at the same time we'd get so far ahead we'd have to wait for them anyway. Besides, it gave us a goal to shoot for. We would see how fast we could pack up and then catch them. I liked the challenge. Pierre *loved* the challenge. He was just finishing tying our supplies into the canoe. I really couldn't help with that. He was very precise about the way the whole thing was done. Today, it hardly seemed necessary. The lake was as calm and smooth as glass, and it wasn't like we were going to be hitting any whitewater. It was just a straight paddle, two or three hours across the lake to the old camp. It had

certainly taken us a lot longer than we'd expected.
I guess a road map wasn't the best indicator of how long
this trip to the camp really took.

"There, all done," he said.

"Great." I started to climb in.

"No," he said, and I stopped mid-step. "Today, you
take the stern."

"Me? You want *me* at the back of the canoe?"

"Are you afraid you can't handle it?" he asked.

"Of course I can!" I said firmly. "It's just that you
always like to be back there. You said that's where the
best canoeist should be."

"Yes, but perhaps the way to become the best is to
take that position and practise." He waded into the
water, towing the canoe by the bow, and jumped in.

I grabbed onto the canoe before it floated away from
me, and hopped in at the back. It wobbled badly for
just a split second, and I had visions of it tipping before
it settled into the water. Yeah, that would have been the
perfect way to start the first time *I* was in control.

Pierre acted as though he hadn't even noticed.
There was no way he wouldn't have, though. He just
didn't say a word. He didn't even turn around.
I appreciated that, because I'm sure the look on his
face would have been hard to disguise.

Instead of worrying I focused on my stroke. I wanted
it to be long and smooth, and to make sure I was keeping

us aimed in the right direction. Nothing wasted more time and energy than a canoe that waddled along, back and forth, like a duck walking along the shore. I needed to keep us in a straight line, like a duck *swimming*.

We were soon making good progress. We weren't moving nearly as fast as we could have with Pierre at the stern, but we'd still pass my mother and sister well before we reached the camp.

I LOOKED UP and there it was—I saw four or five cabins nestled among the trees. A little bit of civilization in the middle of the wilderness. *Very* little. There were bushes growing up all around the buildings, the windows were almost all smashed out, and it looked as though a tree was actually growing up and through the roof of one. The land sloped gently down to a sandy beach. I aimed the canoe toward the beach. It was nice to be the one making the decisions for a change.

The canoe scraped the sandy bottom and both Pierre and I started to get out, one on either side, to balance each other. The bottom was shallow and soft. Pierre towed the canoe up on to the shore, pulling it right out of the water.

I looked up at the camp. I could now see a dozen buildings of different sizes and shapes scattered through the woods. Some were obviously just little log cabins, probably sleeping quarters, and there was one big building in the very centre. Everything was overgrown, but there were paths linking the buildings, marked with little stones that had been painted white and placed as edging. Off in the distance there was a broken-down baseball backstop, rusting and with gaps torn in the mesh. There were hundreds of trees, some taller than the buildings, dotted throughout what had once been the field.

"It's all pretty rundown," I said.

"Nature quickly reclaims what man once owned," Pierre said. "Or thought he owned."

"It's bigger than I thought it would be."

"It was rather magnificent in its time."

I tried to picture what it must have been like. Not just the buildings being in better shape or the bush pushed back, but the kids. I pictured kids running around everywhere, out on the field playing baseball, swimming or lazing on the beach, canoeing out on the lake or just skipping along the path, maybe coming back from a craft activity or a snack. And my father would have been one of those kids. It was almost harder to imagine him being a kid than being a kid up here.

I stopped in front of one of the buildings. It was a single storey tall, constructed with logs, with two windows and a door hanging from one hinge, partway open. I peered in through one of the windows, careful of the broken glass. It was dim inside, but there was enough light to see the wooden skeletons of four sets of bunk beds, stripped of sheets and blankets and mattresses. One was lying on its side and the other three were pushed against the walls. For an instant I thought that the floors were just dirt, but then I saw that there were places where wooden slats were visible beneath a layer of soil that had blown in. In the far corner, where the dirt had gathered, there were mushrooms growing.

"Do you know what happened?" I asked. "Why did it stop being a camp?"

"There was a couple who owned it. They died, and there was nobody to carry on."

"They didn't have any kids?" I asked.

"They probably felt as though they had thousands of kids—the campers—but none who could carry on for them."

"That's sad."

"It is."

He had that thoughtful look that I'd come to recognize. I knew that there were many things on his mind, questions he was trying to answer. I wondered if he was thinking about his son.

"When a man dies, you wonder if his dreams die with him," he said.

"I guess that depends."

"On what?" he asked.

"On the man, the dreams, and who he leaves behind."

He responded with a crooked smile. "Well said."

The sky, which had been getting darker as clouds rolled in, suddenly opened up and it started to sprinkle rain. Just as it did, I could see Jennie and my mother catch up to us, paddling up to the beach, and we ran over to help them land.

"We would be wise to start setting up our camp," Pierre said. "Perhaps, all things considered, we might even consider sleeping indoors tonight."

THE RAIN POUNDED on the cabin roof. It was incredibly loud and it just kept on coming. At least we were inside and dry. Well, sort of inside and sort of dry. The rain was blowing in the broken windows and dripping in from the damaged roof. It wasn't any warmer than if we'd been outside, but it was still a lot drier.

Everybody was sound asleep, my mother and Jennie in one corner and Pierre in another. I really wished I could sleep too. Would I ever sleep through the night again?

Tomorrow we'd scatter the ashes. That was what my mother wanted. What she thought my father would want. It wouldn't make any difference to him, but would it make any difference to any of us?

What might make a difference to me tonight, and help me get to sleep, would be to go to the washroom. I really had to go, and I sure didn't want to go out in the rain and the dark, but what choice did I have?

I pulled my legs out of the sleeping bag and stood up. The room was almost pitch black but there was enough light for me to see the outline of the doorway—the door was partway open and stuck in the dirt at the bottom—and both windows. I grabbed a beat-up roll of toilet paper and started to move along the wall.

"Brian?" It was Pierre. "Is everything all right?"

"Yeah ... I just have to go to the washroom," I whispered.

"Yes ... of course."

I continued moving, one hand against the wall to guide me. I reached the doorway and squeezed through. There was a slight overhang from the roof. A little bit of spray was being blown underneath but I was mostly protected from the rain. I reached out a hand. It was raining but not that hard. As long as I got out and took care of business quickly I wouldn't get too wet. There were some bushes just off to the side. They would have to do.

I sprinted out into the rain. I stopped at the bushes, turned around, dropped my drawers, and crouched down. A quick dump and—I looked over, and there was a little animal right beside me.

I ran forward, my pants still around my ankles, and stumbled, tripping and screaming as I fell face first to the ground.

A little animal, short and squat, groaned and grunted as it waddled off into the bush.

Light appeared in the window of the cabin. I scrambled to pull up my pants.

"Brian!" Pierre yelled as he came through the door, carrying a flashlight.

"It's okay, I'm okay," I said, pulling up my pants and getting to my feet.

"What happened?"

"There was an animal ... it came out of the bushes ... it ran that way."

Pierre trained the light in the direction I had pointed. There was nothing in the beam. Whatever it was, it was gone.

"What sort of animal was it?" he asked.

"Beats me," I said, shaking my head. "It was dark and it just ran by ... it waddled away, grunting and groaning like a pig! I don't know what it was!"

"I think I do. Porcupine. It was probably a porcupine."

"Whatever it was it scared the ... I still have to go to the washroom."

Pierre handed me the flashlight. "Be careful where you squat. It would be embarrassing for both of us if you sat on a porcupine."

He went back into the cabin and I went looking for an unoccupied bush.

IN THE MORNING the camp looked beautiful—the sky was bright blue again, not a cloud in sight, and the rain had left everything looking fresh and glistening. It was hard to feel sombre when everything looked so bright and new—which was probably a good thing, because we had a sombre job to do, and we didn't need to feel any sadder than we already did.

We stood close together at the shoreline, looking out at the lake. Jennie cradled the urn. My mother had an arm around her, as though she was safely guarding her, protecting them both. Jennie handed me the urn and I carefully opened the top. Inside was a plastic bag, and inside of that was all that remained of my father. I undid the little twist tie—it was like opening a loaf of bread. Inside were the ashes, and a little white slip of paper.

I took the slip and unfolded it. It read simply, "Ben Martin—cremated May 6, 1999." I don't know what I'd expected. I guess I'd thought it might say something *more*—I didn't know what, but it seemed to me it should have said *something*. Instead it was just a little label to reassure us that these weren't somebody else's ashes, or ashes from a burned log. How would we even have known if they were?

I slipped the little piece of paper into my pocket and looked at the ashes. They were a fine grey dust, kind of like off-colour baby powder. This was the reason we'd come all the way up here, why we'd risked our lives, why I'd almost drowned. For this. This was all that remained of my father. Somehow it didn't seem right, it didn't seem real.

We stood there looking at each other, uncertain what to do next.

"I thought ...," my mother said. "I thought when the time came, I'd know what to say, but ..."

"May I say a few words?" Pierre suggested.

"Of course." She looked a bit relieved.

He had a solemn look on his face and his eyes looked glassy, watery, as though he was close to tears. He'd told me he always cried at funerals.

Jennie was already in tears. So was my mother. I wasn't.

"Many times, we do not meet the composer, only the music. Many times, we know the artist only by his canvases. Yet in seeing and hearing and feeling the product of the craftsman, we truly know the man who produced that work of art. By the same token, you can know the man by knowing his children.

"I never knew Ben Martin. But I have come to know those people that he loved most, his wife and children. I know he must have been a man of integrity. A man of honesty. A man who possessed a strong sense of pride. And I know that his greatest pride was in his children.

"He was a man who loved the outdoors, who loved his country. I believe that if I had had the good fortune to have met him, we would have been friends."

He looked directly at me. "And I know, I have no doubt, that he is in heaven now." He nodded his head ever so slightly, as though offering me his assurance that it was true. "He is looking down at us and smiling, for he knows that he was loved, and that his family will honour his memory by living their lives in a way that would make him proud."

He paused, and I could see a tear tracing a path down his cheek. And the tears I'd been trying to hide, trying to stop, just came rushing out. My mother slipped her arm around me, as well.

"We have come here not to forget the past, or to destroy the past, but to lay a foundation for the future. Goodbye, Ben. You will be missed."

We walked a few feet forward until we were at the very edge of the water. I took another step until the water was washing over my feet and up my legs. I wasn't sure what to do next. Did we just dump the ashes? That didn't seem right. I gently put my hand into the ashes. They were gritty and rough to the touch.

I closed my fist and pulled it out, and little bits of powder leaked out, dropping into the water. I lifted my hand, opened my fingers, and the ashes fluttered out and dropped to the water. They formed a light film on the surface, and then the little waves overwhelmed them and they were gone, scattered or sunk to the bottom, no different than the sand beneath our toes.

Jennie reached in and took a handful. She held her hand just above the water and released the ashes from just a few inches, as if she didn't want them to break or bruise or get hurt.

My mother went to reach in and then hesitated, holding her hand just above the urn. She took a deep breath, sighed, and then took some of the ashes. She held them in her hand, her fingers squeezed tightly together. She didn't move. It was as though she didn't want to let them go, as though in releasing them she would lose the last bits of my father.

"It's okay, Mom. He's still with us."

She smiled. It was a sad, gentle smile—but it was a smile. She released the ashes and they floated down to the surface of the water.

I took the plastic bag and tipped it over, letting the remaining ashes flutter through the air and into the water. I shook the bag, releasing the last of them. It was empty. Next I bent down and rinsed my hands in the water, washing away the last grains that clung to them. That was it. They were all gone.

All along, I'd wondered why we were really doing this. Would it make any difference? Would it take away that weight that had been on my shoulders, that feeling that so often rested in the pit of my stomach? Suddenly I knew the answer ... I felt free.

CHAPTER FOURTEEN

ONCE AGAIN, Mom and Jennie had set off ahead while Pierre and I packed up. We were now carrying almost all the gear in our canoe.

Today's trip would be pretty straightforward. We were going to do a ten-mile stretch along Cashe Lake, keeping close to the shore, and then down the first five miles or so of the Nappawee River, putting in for the night just before the river entered a series of rapids. The next day we would portage around the rapids. Even thinking about the rapids made me nervous, and I was grateful that we'd be walking around them. Then there'd be another nine or ten miles before we got to a little settlement that Pierre knew about, too small to even be on the map. Pierre knew people who lived there, and he said they could drive us along an old lumber trail, taking us and our gear back around to where our car was waiting. That would be the end of the trip, everything except for the drive home.

I was happy to think about going home—I missed my friends, hot meals, my warm bed, and watching a ball game on TV. I was happy, too, though, that we'd done what we'd set out to do. I suppose, since I'd complained about this trip from the beginning, I should have been just plain happy that it would soon be over. I *did* feel happy, but I was also feeling a little bit sad.

Part of it was the letdown. There was no way this trip could ever have meant all the things my mother thought it should mean. Watching my mother tackle this trip— paddling miles and miles every day with only a little help from Jennie, sleeping on the cold ground, putting up with campfire food and mosquitoes and everything else—I had a new appreciation of how important coming here was to her, and how tough and strong she really was. I missed my dad, but I knew I was lucky to have her on my side. And I knew I was going to be sad to say goodbye to Pierre. He could be annoying, opinionated, brusque, and even rude, but I was going to miss him. Obviously I hadn't known him for very long, but it had been an incredibly intense time, just the two of us in that canoe, or sitting around the fire after my mother and Jennie had gone to sleep.

Pierre was just finishing tying all the gear in the canoe. He was still as annoyingly particular as ever about how everything should be done, but I guess I'd learned to appreciate why he did things his way.

He wasn't always right—even if he thought he was—but he was right so often that I understood why he thought that way.

"Stern or bow?" he asked.

"How about if I start in the stern for the trip across the lake, and then we switch at lunch."

"You mean when we go down the river?" he asked.

"Yeah."

"Are you worried about the rapids?"

"Wasn't even thinking about them," I lied.

"No?" he questioned.

"Not really. Besides, we're going to portage around them, right?"

"That is certainly what we discussed. And I would never allow you to do something you were not prepared for. Shall we go?"

IT TOOK US LESS THAN AN HOUR to catch up with Jennie and my mom, and then we took the lead. I liked being in the lead. Pierre *needed* to be in the lead.

We'd exchanged no more than a dozen words since we'd left. That was okay. It left me time to just *be*. Maybe, I thought, that was one of the many things that people enjoyed about this kind of wilderness trip. I was kind of surprised that I was learning to enjoy quiet and solitude.

"Look," Pierre said, his voice just above a whisper. "Look over there!"

I turned in the direction he was pointing. There was nothing but trees and bush and rocks and ...

"It's a moose!" I exclaimed.

"Sshhh!"

There in the shallow water, no more than fifty feet away, stood a gigantic moose. It had an enormous rack of antlers and a long, furry, brown coat. It dipped its head under the water right up to the antlers. Then it pulled its head up and there were plants hanging out of its mouth. It lazily chewed.

"It's enormous," I said.

It continued to chew. It looked like a large cow with velvety antlers. It looked up, in our direction, with large, brown, liquid eyes.

"He's looking for the sound," Pierre said. "Poor eyesight but wonderful hearing."

It seemed to be able to focus on Pierre's voice and it looked directly at us.

"Can we get closer?" I asked.

Pierre shook his head. "This is close enough. Moose can be dangerous."

I chuckled. "It doesn't look dangerous. It looks like a big cow."

"It is actually a bull moose and it weighs over six hundred kilograms—that's about thirteen hundred pounds. It can kill a wolf with one swipe of its front hooves or a charge with its antlers. And it can easily outrun a man or out-swim a canoe."

It suddenly didn't seem so funny. I no longer wanted to get closer. Maybe a little extra water between us and it would be a good thing.

Pierre clapped his hands and both the moose and I startled. It froze, mid-chew. Pierre clapped his hands again and it turned and ran, splashing through the water, charging up onto the shore, and then crashed through the brush, snapping off branches until it disappeared into the forest. Although I couldn't see it any longer, I could still hear it smashing its way through the trees.

"Why did you do that?"

"I wanted it gone before your mother and Jennie arrive. It seemed wise."

That did make sense.

"This is why I like to lead. You can see more but be aware of possible dangers for those who follow."

"Are you sure it won't come back?"

"By now it is half a mile away in the forest. It will not return. As big and strong as it is, a moose prefers to avoid confrontation or contact when possible."

PIERRE STOPPED PADDLING and turned slightly around in his seat. "We have company."

"Company? Is the moose back?" I looked all around for a swimming moose plowing through the water toward us.

"Not a moose. A canoe."

I peered around him, searching, and then I saw it. There was a canoe coming across the lake. It was almost like an optical illusion. I could see it—a bright red canoe standing out against the dark blue water— but I could hardly believe my eyes. We hadn't seen anyone else since we'd met Pierre, so it seemed incredibly strange to just run into somebody out here in the middle of nowhere. Then again, that's how we'd run into Pierre.

We angled our canoe toward their approach. Pierre lifted up his paddle and waved it above his head. The man in the bow waved back. They'd seen us—two men dressed in clothing almost as bright as their canoe. We watched as they got closer and closer.

"Who do you think they are?" I asked.

He shrugged. "Not locals."

"How can you tell?"

"By their dress. They're from down south."

"*Bonjour!*" one of the men yelled out.

"*Bonjour! Comment ça va?*" Pierre yelled back. He turned to me. "French Canadians."

The canoe glided right in beside us and Pierre grabbed its side to hold it there. They started to speak in French, and then the first man suddenly stopped, mid-sentence. His eyes widened, as if he was in shock. His stared, open-mouthed, at Pierre. I looked at the second man—his expression was the same. What was wrong? What had Pierre said to them that had shocked them so badly?

Pierre spoke and they unfroze. The first man lurched forward and grabbed Pierre's hand and started pumping it vigorously up and down. The second guy jumped up, rocking his canoe and ours so badly that for a split second I thought we were both going to tip over. He started speaking to Pierre excitedly, taking his hand in both of his and shaking it up and down, up and down. They were practically bowing their heads, bobbing them up and down, and although I didn't understand a word they were saying they seemed awfully excited about something. Maybe they knew each other, or maybe that was just the way French people were. Often the Spanish-speaking people I knew were like that when they met.

Pierre gestured to me and then said something to them in French—the only thing I understood was my name. The first man shook my hand. He was all smiles.

"So pleased," he said in a heavily accented voice.

"Me too," I mumbled back.

The second man shook my hand. He nodded his head, smiled, and spoke to me in French. He could have been saying anything, but he was smiling, so it couldn't have been too bad.

They began speaking to Pierre again in rapid-fire French. There was lots of gesturing, and Pierre pointed back in the direction we had just come. He must have been offering them directions or some information. They certainly seemed pretty happy with whatever he was telling them.

I tried to pick out some of the words. My father had always said that French, English, and Spanish had a lot of words in common. I knew I could sometimes pick out a word or two when I heard people speaking Spanish. There were words that I thought I understood.

Finally they shook hands with Pierre again, and then they reached over to shake my hand, as well.

"You ... you ... so ... fortunate," one man said, pumping my hand up and down. "To be ... with..." He gestured to Pierre.

"Thanks," I mumbled. I wished I had some idea what he was talking about.

I released their canoe and we pushed off. They started paddling and yelled out what I assumed was goodbye as they moved off.

"Did you know them?" I asked.

Pierre shook his head.

"They seemed awfully glad to meet you."

"It is rare to run into somebody up here. They would have been happy to meet anybody."

"Yeah, I guess."

We began paddling. That could have been it … no … it was more than that. They weren't that happy to meet *me*.

"I think there must be something else," I said.

"French Canadians are very friendly people."

"Not that friendly, and that isn't it." They were practically bowing their heads, and the one guy had almost capsized their canoe in his rush to shake hands with Pierre. "It was like it was a really big deal for them to meet you, like you were somebody *important*."

He shrugged, but didn't answer. There was more there—I was sure of it now—but while he wasn't going to lie, he clearly wasn't going to tell me, either.

PIERRE CAME BACK from the river where he'd washed up the supper dishes. It had taken him a while to get the frying pan clean. We'd had fish for supper. Talk about fresh! Less than thirty minutes from the river to our stomachs. Pierre had caught them, cleaned them, cooked them, and now was doing all the washing. My mother had offered to help, but he had insisted on doing it himself.

He joined us around the campfire. Our last campfire. Our last night. By this time tomorrow we'd be in our car driving home. The night after that we'd be safe in our condo in Manhattan, a million miles from here. This whole trip would be nothing more than a memory.

My mother had an arm around Jennie and the two of them were wrapped in a blanket. It was getting chilly. We had dragged the two canoes up close to the fire, angling them so we'd get some warmth until the embers died.

"It's a beautiful night," my mother said.

"It is," Pierre agreed.

"I'm sad it's almost over," she said. "What are you two going to miss the most?"

"Me?" I asked. "I guess sleeping outdoors under the stars." The only people who slept outdoors in New York were street people, and while there were surely stars somewhere up in the skies, they were hidden by the lights of the city.

"And you, Jennie?" my mother asked.

She didn't answer right away. She shook her head. "Everything."

"How about you, Mom?" I asked.

"I think I'll miss being alone. In New York there are always tens of thousands, hundreds of thousands of people all around you all the time. Here, it's just us."

"Well, not today," I said. "That was pretty strange running into those other canoeists." I wasn't ready to let this one go. "They were really friendly, weren't they?"

They had run across my mother and Jennie after we'd met up with them.

"They seemed friendly enough," my mother said.

"They were really, *really* friendly with us," I said. "It was like they were excited to meet Pierre. They acted like he was a celebrity. They were practically bowing, and the way that one guy almost tipped the canoe trying to shake your hand..."

Pierre just shrugged.

"Wait," my mother said. "Pierre ... your last name ... what *is* your last name?"

He paused for a moment, then, "Trudeau. Pierre Elliott Trudeau."

"Oh my goodness ... Trudeau," my mother said, her voice barely a whisper. "Oh my goodness."

"What is it? What's wrong?" I asked anxiously.

She looked at me, wide-eyed. "He's Pierre Trudeau."

Yeah, he'd just said that was his name. So what?

"My husband used to talk about you," she gasped.

"Pierre knew Dad?" I asked. How could that be possible?

"No," she said, shaking her head. "Pierre didn't know your father, but your father knew Pierre, I mean Mr. Trudeau. He was the prime minister of Canada."

"I don't know what that means," I said. "What's a prime minister?"

"It's like the president of the United States," my mother said.

I looked at him. "You ran the whole country?"

He shrugged. "As I said, I worked for the government."

"You didn't work for the government. You *were* the government."

"A small part, and many years ago."

"Why didn't you tell us?" I asked.

"It didn't seem important," he said. "What difference would it have made if you had known?"

"Well…" I didn't have an answer. It wouldn't have made any difference at all. "But still, you should have told us."

"In hindsight, I suppose I should have. It might have been more polite, more honest." He paused. "It is just that it is difficult sometimes to have people react in a certain way."

"Like those two guys in the canoe?" I asked.

He nodded. "It is unnecessary … embarrassing. You did not know who I was, and I enjoyed simply being Pierre. My apologies, my *deepest* apologies if I have offended you in any way."

"Of course you didn't offend us!" my mother exclaimed. "We're just so grateful you were there. I don't know what we would have done without you. And to think, I didn't even know who you are!"

It seemed to me as if something *had* changed, though. It was hard for me to see Pierre the same way. I had thought he was probably just some retired guy on a camping trip ... which, I guess, he was. But now I knew he was something else, too ... somebody really important. I hoped he wouldn't feel strange, now that we knew. I hoped we could just go on the same way. But he seemed a bit uncomfortable all of a sudden, a bit more stiff and formal.

"It was truly my pleasure." He stood up. "And now, it is time for me to retire. Good night."

Pierre had never been the first to leave the campfire and go to bed. Something had definitely changed.

CHAPTER FIFTEEN

PIERRE WAS CROUCHED on his haunches, facing toward the river. It was early enough that the morning mist was still hovering above the water. I came up slowly, quietly, trying not to disturb him. He continued to stare into the distance and I continued to stand, waiting. And as I waited I watched the river, too.

We were camped out on a small plateau just at the beginning of the rapids. This was the point where the quiet, gentle river we'd paddled on turned into a monster. There were gigantic rocks breaking the surface, and white, foaming water rushed around them. The river twisted, and I could see drops and dips along the whole stretch before it cut sharply to the right and out of sight. Who knew what it would be like from that point on?

Finally, Pierre turned around and stood up.

"Good morning," he said.

"Morning. I didn't mean to disturb you."

"You didn't."

"Were you meditating?" I asked.

He shook his head. "Just looking at the river. I suppose, in a way, it's the same thing."

"Those rapids are something else," I said. "I've been staring at them too."

"And?" Pierre asked.

"And I think those are even bigger than the ones I body-surfed through."

"Longer. Not necessarily bigger. Certainly not as dangerous."

"Really?"

"Yes, I am sure. You slept well last night?" Pierre asked.

"Yeah, I did," I agreed. "I slept right through the night."

"You sound surprised ... and pleased."

"Both. I just hope it won't be the only night."

"We can both hope." He put his hand on my shoulder. "I also hope that I am forgiven for not telling your family about who I am."

"There's nothing to be forgiven for. You were right, it didn't matter, and I guess I even understand why you did it."

"You do?"

"Probably people bug you all the time, treat you differently. You just wanted to be left alone. That's why you came up here by yourself, right? To be left alone?"

"When you are in the public eye, it feels as though you no longer belong to yourself. Up here, I am myself."

"That makes sense to me." I chuckled. "You really were the prime minister."

"I had that honour."

"I was just curious, shouldn't you have a bunch of bodyguards with you, or Mounties or something? Shouldn't they be lurking in the woods, watching you all the time?"

"I had bodyguards when I was the prime minister. But if they were with me on this trip I would be taking care of them. Rather than lurking in the woods they would be lost in the woods, and you and I would have to find them."

I laughed.

"I was prime minister a long time ago."

"But in the States even former presidents always have Secret Service agents with them, all the time," I said.

"This is Canada. I have no need for the Secret Service."

"You know, it's just strange to think that you ran this whole country."

"Many times it seemed as though the country ran me ... but I attempted to share my ideas and my ideals with Canada. I wanted to make a difference."

"And?"

He paused for a moment. "I believe I had some impact." He stood up and took a deep breath. "Isn't the air wonderful?"

"A lot fresher than what I'm going to be breathing tomorrow back in NYC. But before that happens we have a long drive, and before that a long portage carrying all our equipment."

"The car ride is unavoidable, but perhaps the difficult portage is not."

"What do you mean?"

"I have decided to go through the rapids," Pierre said.

"But you can't do that … you *can't* … there's no way you could get through that," I said, pointing at the whitewater.

"I have gone through these rapids before."

"You have?"

"On two occasions."

I looked at the river and then back at him. That was hard to believe, but I knew he must be telling the truth.

"You could come with me … if you wish."

"What?"

"You could come through the rapids with me."

"You're kidding … right?" He had to be kidding.

"No." He said the word quietly, calmly, matter-of-factly.

A chill went up my spine. He really wanted me to do it. I had a feeling this was one of those getting-back-on-the-horse things.

"Of course, you can portage if you wish. It is up to you."

I let out a little sigh of relief. Okay, he wasn't going to *make* me do it … it was my choice … my choice to walk … my choice to take a chance.

"You really think I could do it … you think I could shoot the rapids?"

"You know I would never ask you to do something that you were not capable of. You could shoot the rapids … *we* could shoot the rapids."

I looked at the river, at the rapids, and then turned back toward Pierre.

"Do you want me to be in the bow or the stern?"

"AND YOU'RE SURE he'll be all right?" my mother said.

"I'll be fine." I was trying very hard to convince both of us. "We'll be safe."

"I wish I could be sure," she said.

"There are no certainties," Pierre said. "There is always a degree of risk."

Was he trying to talk her into this or me out of it? This wasn't the pep talk I was hoping for.

"If you would rather, then he will portage around the rapids with you," Pierre said.

I looked anxiously at my mother. I didn't know what I should hope she'd say. If she said no, then I wouldn't go, but it wouldn't be because I wasn't brave. I'd have an excuse. But I also wouldn't be able to go, and I wanted to go. Well, at least the biggest chunk of me ... it was probably a 51–49 split.

"And you're sure ... you think he'll be fine?" my mother asked, repeating the original question in slightly different words.

"Your son is a remarkable young man," he said. "To be willing to attempt a set of rapids so soon after his misfortune is a sign of strength, integrity. I have every faith in him, in me, in our canoe, and in our paddles."

I almost started to blush. That was more like what I wanted him to say. I trusted Pierre and he trusted me. That was good enough for me.

"Please, Mom," I said.

She nodded, and then threw her arms around me and gave me a big hug.

"You and Jennie should proceed down the river. You'll find a good spot about four hundred yards down where you'll be able to see us shooting the rapids," Pierre said.

My mother squeezed a little harder and then released me. They put on their packs, she took Jennie by the hand, and they started down the path. I watched them until they were out of sight. She didn't look back.

"Right, then. Let's review our strategy," Pierre said.

He had walked down the river that morning and surveyed the rapids, and then explained it all to me. He crouched down now over a sandy stretch of ground. There in the sand was a crudely drawn map of the river. He pointed at a spot.

"Tell me about the first rapids we'll encounter," he said.

"Again?" We'd already gone through this twice.

"Again, until you can give it to me error free."

"But I'm not even in the stern."

"Regardless, you need to know our exact route."

There was no point in arguing. Not just because he was right, but because he was Pierre. I didn't think anybody could argue with him and win.

I picked up a stick and pointed at the spot. "Right here—unless they've moved since we went through this the last time—there are rocks sticking out in the centre of the river. There's a drop, maybe two feet, and we can pass on either side, but we're going to pass on the left side."

"Because?" he asked.

"Because here," I said, pointing farther down, "is another set of rapids that is passable only on the left, so we'll need to be on that side of the river."

"Good. Now continue."

"From here down there are lots of dips, none too big, but there are rocks that are big enough to smash the canoe. I'm supposed to yell out what I see."

He nodded his head. "Continue."

"Then there's one more big drop. We have to take it on the right-hand side because that's the best passage."

"Correct. And then?"

"Then there's flat water for at least a hundred yards before the rapids begin again."

"And in that section there are three or four places where we can set the canoe in if we choose not to go through the next set."

"You mean if *I* choose not to go through."

"If either of us makes that decision the other will honour it. That is the pact that is always made between two partners in a canoe. Please go on."

"The second set of rapids isn't as bad as the first. We just have to stay to the right-hand side all the way down, until we get to the big drop. We have to go over the drop in the middle."

"Excellent."

It was reassuring to realize that I knew the route so well. Of course, that was the only thing that was reassuring about the whole adventure.

Pierre stood up and I trailed him to the canoe. It was sitting on the shore, waiting for us. Pierre reached out and tightened the belt on my life jacket. Maybe that should have made me feel better. It didn't.

I waded into the water and helped pull the canoe into the water. The bottom dropped off quickly and I jumped in before it got too deep. Pierre was still in the shallows, holding the canoe in place.

"Ready?" he asked.

I nodded.

"You don't need to do this," he said.

"Yes I do."

"You do not have to prove anything to me," Pierre said.

"I know. It's not you I'm doing it for. What about you? You're the one who doesn't need to do it. You've done it before."

"Well, yes … but that was over forty-five years ago."

"Wow … that was a long…." I let the sentence trail off.

"Yes, it was a long time ago. But at least that time I made it all the way down without mishap."

"Mishap?"

"The first time I went through these rapids I capsized going over the last drop."

"If you're trying to convince me that we can do this you're doing a really crummy job."

"I am not trying to convince you to do anything. It is your choice." He paused. "And?"

"Get in the canoe," I said.

He smiled, then jumped in.

Almost immediately I could feel the current capture the canoe. The canoe picked up speed fast. We were heading for the rapids. This was it. There was no going back now. I grabbed my paddle and dipped it in. I started to paddle hard on the right side, digging in, trying to help move to the left side.

The first whitewater came into view and the sound of the rapids grew louder and louder. The banks were rising up on both sides and the river narrowed. The water was funnelled, picking up more and more speed. The canoe dipped slightly. Before I could react we'd dropped down the first drop. Cold water splashed into my face and I tried to stifle the scream as my stomach rose up into my throat. The canoe bounced and rocked, and for a split second I thought we were going to tip before we settled down. We were picking up more speed—or maybe it just seemed that way because we were so close to the left bank, which rose sharply up. We hit a little bump, and then another and another. It was like a little roller coaster . . . This wasn't so . . . The river dropped off, like falling off a cliff! We went straight down! The bow of the canoe was buried and water streamed in over me!

I closed my eyes and my mouth and wedged my legs under the seat to pin me in place. I was staying with this canoe no matter where it was going ... even if it was going ... The canoe levelled out ... We were through it!

"Dig! Dig! Dig!" Pierre yelled.

I snapped back to life and dug in with my paddle ... no, I was paddling on the wrong side! I flipped the paddle around and started paddling hard on the left side ... we had to get over to the far right side of the river. The canoe shot forward and then sideways as we cut sharply across the current. We bounced over some smaller dips, and then a big dip, and then we straightened out, just as we hit the next drop. The canoe plummeted down and I screamed before the cascade of water forced me to close my mouth. We bucked and bounced and then settled down and slowed down. I took a long, deep breath and looked around. The river had widened, the banks had flattened, and the water had slowed down dramatically. We were through the first section! We settled into a little backwater, off to the side, out of the current.

"Excellent work, Brian, excellent!" Pierre exclaimed.

There was cheering from the shore and I startled. My mother and sister were standing on a large rock screaming and waving and jumping up and down. I waved back, even though I felt embarrassed—and happy.

Actually, *happy* wasn't the right word. My whole body was tingling as if there were ripples of electricity running through it, and my head felt like it was buzzing.

"How do you feel?" Pierre asked.

"Good ... no ... great!"

"*Nothing is so exhilarating as being shot at and missed.*"

"What?"

"Winston Churchill. To survive something dangerous creates a marvellous feeling."

"That *is* how I'm feeling."

"Excellent. So do we put in or do we go on?"

I didn't even have to think. "We go on."

He nodded and smiled. "First we must bail the water out of the canoe."

I suddenly realized that the canoe was almost completely filled. In the excitement I hadn't even noticed. My feet and my legs were submerged and the water was almost as high as the seat.

Pierre handed me a plastic cup. He took one himself and we both started bailing. I worked as hard as I could. I wanted to get to the next section. Not because I wanted to get it over with, but because I just wanted to do it.

"Is that good enough?" I asked.

"A little more."

"But won't it just fill up again as we go through the next section?"

"Perhaps, but we need to be light so we can stay on the top, be more buoyant. Keep bailing."

I wanted to go, but I wasn't going to argue. I worked even faster until finally the water was just between the ribs on the bottom of the canoe.

"Now?" I asked impatiently.

"And you know our route?"

"I do. Want me to tell you?"

"No. I trust you."

We started paddling. The canoe nosed out and was instantly spun by the current, which was pointing it downstream. Quickly we gained speed and I could see the first of the whitewater looming up ahead. My confidence started to wilt.

"This section isn't as bad … right?" I yelled over my shoulder.

"Not as bad."

"That's good to——"

"Except for the falls," he said, cutting me off.

Right, the falls. That was the last drop, the end of the rapids before we were through. But it wasn't really a waterfall, it was just a big drop. We'd be okay. Now, as the river captured us, nothing really mattered. We were going, whether we wanted to or not.

We dipped down over the first drop and water sprayed up into my face. I felt that same burst of electricity surge through me. We were tucked in close to the shore and we shot through a gap between the shore and the rocks that dotted the river. All we had to do was keep on this route and—

"Rocks! Rocks! Straight ahead!" I screamed.

I swung my paddle around, flipping it to the left side to try to move us—we hit against a rock! I almost fell out as the impact bounced us to the side. Before I could even react there were more rocks jutting out directly in front of us.

"Right! Right! Right! We have to go to the right!" I yelled.

The canoe shot forward but moved to the right, and the canoe grazed the rocks as we shot by.

There was no time to think before there were more rocks, more rapids, more whitewater. It seemed as though there was no way through, as if the whole river was blocked—there was a gap! We just had to go straight.

Suddenly the canoe jammed against one of the rocks and I fell forward, landing on the bottom while the canoe stood still! We were stuck, we were jammed into some rocks in the river in the middle of the rapids! No ... we weren't stuck ... we were moving ... *sideways*.

The current captured the stern of the canoe and we started to turn, perpendicular to the river. For a second it looked as though the rocks were going to hold us in place, and then they gave way, and the whole canoe spun around, and I was facing upstream while we were racing downstream … we were going backwards through the rapids!

Terrified, I looked over my shoulder in the direction we were moving. Pierre was churning the water with his paddle, trying desperately to turn us back around. He hadn't given up and neither could I. I summoned up the rush of electricity surging through me and dug in my paddle.

"The other side!" Pierre yelled. "Dig in your paddle on the other side!"

For a split second it didn't register what he meant, then I understood. I flipped around the paddle and dug in on the other side. The canoe started to turn, but it was fighting against the force of the current, which was trying to keep us aimed backwards. The canoe dipped again—that was even more terrifying because I didn't see it coming.

"Harder!" Pierre yelled.

I turned the paddle and we started to pivot. While we raced downriver we slowly turned until we were sideways, and then the water caught us and swung us around—we were facing the right direction again! I could see the river in front of us—I could see where the river *disappeared*. We were on the verge of the big drop.

We bounced and rocked and then shot over the drop. For a split second I had the strange illusion that we were actually flying. Then I felt as if I were in an elevator plummeting to the basement from the top floor. We dropped, nose first, and the whole world exploded in cold water as the canoe sliced into the water. The water washed over me, like a wave, practically dragging me out of the canoe, and then ... it was over.

We glided forward across the water. I was soaked to the bone and I was sitting in a bathtub full of water, but we were through. We'd shot the falls and survived. And I had a great feeling—that feeling you sometimes get when you know that, for whatever reason, you are exactly where you are supposed to be.

Mom and Jennie were racing down to meet us, yelling and cheering the whole way!

Pierre reached forward and slapped me on the back. I turned around. There was a glint in his eye, and he had a small, quirky smile.

He didn't say a word. He didn't need to.

CHAPTER SIXTEEN

JENNIE, MY MOTHER, AND I sat on the bumper of the pickup truck. It was beaten up, really old, had more rust than paint, and the windshield was a spiderweb of cracks. We'd just finished stowing our canoe and gear in the back. From the looks of that truck I was thinking that the drive back to our car might be more dangerous than my trip over the rapids ... *the rapids*. I'd done it. I didn't think there was one thing I'd done in my whole life that had ever made me feel so proud. My father would have been proud of me, too. That thought made me sad, but it also made me happy.

Pierre came out of a little house along with its owner, the man who was going to drive us. The two of them were laughing and joking like a couple of old friends—actually, they were old friends. Pierre told us he'd known Jacques since they were both in their teens.

"Well, are you all packed?" Pierre asked.

"Everything is in," I said.

"It's going to be a very bumpy ride. Is it all tied down properly?"

"Brian took care of that," my mother replied.

Pierre nodded his head. "Then I know it is done correctly."

"Guess we'd better get moving," Jacques said.

"In which case, we should be saying our goodbyes," Pierre said.

This was it. We were going back to our car, back to New York, and Pierre was going back to his canoe to continue his own trip. This was the end.

"I don't know how we can ever thank you," my mother said. She wrapped her arms around him and gave him a big hug.

"No thanks are necessary. It was my pleasure."

Pierre walked over to Jennie. She was still sitting on the truck's bumper, staring at nothing. I knew she was on the verge of crying. She was fighting hard to keep the tears in but was starting to lose the fight.

Pierre bent down so they were face to face. "I will miss you, Jennie," he said.

She looked down at the ground. "I'll miss you, too."

He reached out and put his hand gently under her chin, lifting her head up. "There is nothing wrong with tears." With the other hand he brushed away a tear that was falling down her cheek.

"I don't want to say goodbye," she said, her voice cracking over the last word.

"Then let's not say goodbye. Let's just say, '*À la prochaine fois*.'"

"What does that mean?" Jennie asked.

"It means, 'Until we meet again.'"

She threw her arms around Pierre's neck and gave him a big hug. He put his mouth close to her ear and said something ... I couldn't hear what he was saying, but she burst into laughter. She released her grip and ran over to our mother, who was standing at the door of the truck.

He stood up and turned to me. "I believe you forgot to pack one thing."

"I did? What?"

"Your paddle."

"I lost my paddle, remember?"

"Not the one you lost. The one you used ... the one I lent you."

"But that's your paddle."

"It *was* my paddle. Now it is yours."

"I can't do that. It's your spare. You can't go back out there without an extra paddle."

"I've loaned him another one," Jacques said.

"Come." Pierre turned and started walking back down the path to the river, toward his canoe. I trotted behind and caught up.

"You must be looking forward to getting home," Pierre said.

"I'm looking forward to a soft bed, and seeing my friends, but ... I don't know."

"You don't know what?" he asked.

"This is going to sound strange, but it feels like this is an okay place to be, too."

"That doesn't sound strange at all. A man can have more than one place where he feels that he belongs. Just like a man can be more than one thing. I hope the paddle will help you to remember that."

"I don't need the paddle to remember. You really don't have to give it to me," I said.

"I'm not giving it to you. You *earned* it. It is yours."

We stopped at the canoe. He reached down and picked up the paddle. He held it up and slowly turned it around, looking at it. It was beautiful.

"It is a fine paddle." He handed it to me.

It felt right in my hands.

"May you use it on many trips to come. Perhaps you will even return here one day."

"Would you join me if I did?"

He didn't answer right away. "Your future is all ahead of you. I am old. My life is almost all behind me. This could be my last trip." He reached out and put a hand on the paddle. "But you have to promise me that this paddle will be used." He looked me straight in the eyes—staring, strong, unblinking. He was serious.

"I promise."

He released the paddle.

"I know I'll come back here again," I said.

"That would make your father happy," Pierre said. "It's a way of remembering him."

"That's one of the reasons you came, isn't it ... to remember your son."

"I came for the solitude and for the time to think." He paused. "But also to both remember and honour my son."

I knew exactly what he meant. Exactly.

"Thank you for the paddle," I said.

He shook his head. "Perhaps I should thank you."

"Me? I didn't do anything."

"You did more than you think."

He held out his hand and we shook.

"I was the guide, but you helped move *both* of us forward." He released my hand. "Now we both must go."

He waded into the water and towed his canoe behind him until it was floating. He climbed in. He aimed the canoe upriver and started paddling. I watched as with each strong stroke he moved farther and farther away, fighting against the current, but winning. I waited, hoping he'd look back, but he didn't. He rounded the curve and disappeared. He was gone, but he'd never be forgotten.

AUTHOR'S NOTE

FOR A MAN WHO VOICED the need for reason over passion, Trudeau was the Canadian political leader most synonymous with passion. His ideas, his politics, and his life created powerful emotions, actions, and reactions in the people of this country. And while he is often remembered for his style, the substance of the man is so much more significant. The rose, the pirouette, and the convertible mean little compared to his vision, intellect, and determination. He saw what Canada was, knew what it could become, and through the sheer power of his person, he transformed this country. Whether he is loved or loathed—and he inspires those extremes—his impact on the country and his place as one of Canada's most influential figures is indisputable. Sir John A. Macdonald founded this country; Trudeau's influence allowed Canada to remain intact.

While Trudeau can be justifiably accused of being, at times, stubborn, arrogant, and rude, he also possessed incredible sensitivity, understanding, gentleness, and a true spirit of caring for those most in need. He was, I believe, at his very best in the company of children, while in a canoe, and when teaching. This novel is an intersection of those three situations.

In writing a novel that includes as a character a real person known to all Canadians, it is essential to be as accurate as possible in presenting Mr. Trudeau. I did extensive research, aided in part by reading all the books suggested to me by his son Justin Trudeau. Many words spoken by my character were actually voiced by Trudeau in speeches or written by him in essays.

I hope you can become more knowledgable about the person behind the legend, a man I would have been honoured to have shared a canoe with—of course, with him in the stern.